Time was running out.

Katherine rushed to the door, cracked it open and peeked out just as the two men stepped off the elevator at the other end of the hall. They were still too far away to identify, but she knew they were after her and Randy.

She closed the door and hurried to Randy's bedside. "No time to explain. We've got to move. Fast. And we've got to be quiet. Our lives depend on it."

Randy gritted his teeth and jerked the IV needle out of his arm. He gestured for her to unplug the vital signs monitor, and then he disentangled himself from all the wires and reached over to power off the monitor before the battery backup could set off the alarm. Katherine watched in awe as he took a deep breath and stood, confident and strong, even though he had to be in excruciating pain.

Her mind raced, trying to hit on an idea that would help them make their escape. She had to think fast, or they'd both be dead...

Rhonda Starnes is a retired middle school language arts teacher who dreamed of being a published author from the time she was in seventh grade and wrote her first short story. She lives in North Alabama with her husband, who she lovingly refers to as Mountain Man. They enjoy traveling and spending time with their children and grandchildren. Rhonda writes heart-and-soul suspense with rugged heroes and feisty heroines.

Books by Rhonda Starnes

Love Inspired Suspense

Rocky Mountain Revenge
Perilous Wilderness Escape

Visit the Author Profile page at LoveInspired.com.

PERILOUS WILDERNESS ESCAPE

RHONDA STARNES

LOVE INSPIRED SUSPENSE
INSPIRATIONAL ROMANCE

LOVE INSPIRED® SUSPENSE
INSPIRATIONAL ROMANCE

ISBN-13: 978-1-335-72310-9

Recycling programs for this product may not exist in your area.

Perilous Wilderness Escape

Copyright © 2022 by Rhonda L. Starnes

For questions and comments about the quality of this book, please contact us at CustomerService@Harlequin.com.

Love Inspired
22 Adelaide St. West, 41st Floor
Toronto, Ontario M5H 4E3, Canada
www.LoveInspired.com

Printed in U.S.A.

The Lord is far from the wicked:
but he heareth the prayer of the righteous.
—*Proverbs* 15:29

To my siblings, Renae, Randy and Kristy. I love you all!

In loving memory of my mother-in-law, Evelyn. I can still hear your laughter. You are dearly missed!

Acknowledgments

Glenda and Booge, thank you for letting Mountain Man use your attic ladder to test my belt trick idea.

Sarah, your back patio is such a lovely space. Thank you for allowing me to use it as my writing oasis when I had family visiting and needed a quiet place to work.

A special thank-you to my editor, Tina James.
I am blessed to work with you.
Thank you for all of your guidance.

ONE

"You have reached the—"

Voice mail. Again. FBI Agent Randy Ingalls gripped the steering wheel tighter. This was his fourth attempt to reach his partner. Most people he knew were practically glued to their phones, but not Agent Katherine Lewis. She never seemed to have her phone handy, or at least not when he needed to get in touch with her.

They were paired together after his partner of five years, Agent Trevor Douglas, died in a horrific car crash. In the eleven months Randy and Katherine had worked together, he'd lost count of the number of times he'd experienced frustration over not being able to reach her. He really needed to find out how she was spending her time on the days she worked from home—if the run-down, two-bedroom house with minimal furnishings they were using while on assignment could be called home. No matter what he called their living quarters, his partner was always eager to stay behind and do any computer work or research that needed to be done.

Oh well, nothing left to do but leave a message and pray Lewis being MIA was simply a case of a dead battery. The automated voice finished its spiel and the beep sounded.

"Lewis, I overheard Torres on the phone with his mysterious boss discussing a plan to meet tonight. I'm following Torres and his goon right now. This could be the break we've been looking for." Lightning flashed in the distance, and large raindrops started pelting the windshield. Great. A late-April thunderstorm was the last thing he needed at the moment. He flipped on the wipers. "As a precaution, you need to clear out of the rental. Take everything with you. Wait for me at our designated safe place. If I'm not there by midnight, call SAC Richardson for backup."

He disconnected the call. Putting a person's life in danger without their knowledge—even another agent who knew risks were part of the job—wasn't something he liked to do. Unfortunately, when Randy had overheard Torres's phone conversation this evening, he'd needed to act quickly and hadn't had time to go back to the rental to fill Lewis in on what was happening. Hopefully, she would hear his message sooner rather than later.

Randy could picture her listening to his message. The cell phone pressed to her ear, she'd play with a strand of her long, wavy brown hair and a frown would pucker her brow as she mentally calculated all that needed to be done to follow his command, including—he sucked in his breath—securing transportation to the safe location.

He'd taken off in their only vehicle without a second thought. Too late to do anything about it now. Besides, Agent Lewis may not keep her phone handy, but she was very resourceful. She'd be fine. He hoped.

Puffing out the breath, he focused on the road ahead. The dark gray Jeep he'd been tailing for the past forty-five minutes was about a hundred yards ahead of him. He pressed down on the gas pedal, desperate to keep the vehicle in sight as they approached the curvier mountainous terrain.

The antique A-11 military watch on his left wrist caught his attention, and he turned his arm so he could see the face. 7:43 p.m. How many times had he heard the story of the watch? Hundreds, he was sure. The watch had belonged to Trevor and had been one of his most prized possessions. Now it was Randy's. A gift from Trevor a few days before his death. Randy's throat tightened, and he hit the steering wheel.

"I won't let them get away this time, Trevor. Promise. I'll shut down their illegal activities and prove they were behind your accident. They will be brought to justice for your murder." Randy made the vow to his dead partner, the same as he had multiple times since he'd found Trevor's mangled, burning vehicle at the bottom of a ravine.

The sun sank farther below the horizon, the last streaks of orange and gold quickly disappearing, leaving behind ominous darkness, the stars and moon blocked by the storm clouds that had rolled in.

Though he had no clue where they were going when they left Dove Creek—a small town about twenty miles north of Laramie—it hadn't surprised him when they crossed over into Colorado. After all, the illegal match races had originated there, bouncing all around the state before moving to Wyoming.

Randy had been trying to bust the illegal horse racing ring with suspected ties to a Mexican drug cartel for the better part of two years. He had come close ten months ago when Torres and his men had set up operations southwest of Colorado Springs near the small town of Blackberry Falls, but Torres had given them the slip when Lewis had left her lookout post to aid the local police chief in protecting his witness.

It had taken seven months to locate the operation again and another two months for him and Lewis to get undercover jobs with the organization. Randy would not let Torres get away this time. It was time to put these evil men behind bars. And, as his grandpa Ingalls had taught him, to eliminate an invasive weed, the roots have to be pulled out, too. That's why Randy wanted to take down not only Torres and the goons working for him, but also the elusive behind-the-scenes boss man.

How much farther until they reached their destination? A shiver ran up his spine, and he cranked up the heat a few degrees. Maybe he should try Lewis again. It wouldn't be a bad idea to let his partner know he'd left Wyoming. If only he had taken the time to download the tracking app on their phones last week, like he'd intended to do, then Randy wouldn't have to worry about her knowing his location.

He pressed the call button on the steering wheel as he watched the faint red taillights go around the curve up ahead. The call went straight to voice mail. Frustrated, he hung up. He would try later.

The rain was coming down in sheets now, impeding his ability to see. He accelerated as much as he dared. They'd reached the point in the journey where he needed to close the gap between them or risk losing the other vehicle. The rainstorm along with the recently melted snow made the trip even more treacherous, with the added risk of mudslides and downed trees.

Rounding the curve, he found the Jeep. Stopped. Alongside a big, dark-colored SUV, at a pull-off on the shoulder of the road, doors open and lights off on both vehicles. The SUV faced his direction, parked half on and half off the road.

Randy was going to hit them. He slammed on the brake pedal, straining to control the skid as the tires fought for traction on the slick pavement. His vehicle spun around and around. Then the sound of rock scraping against metal echoed in the silence of the night as his SUV brushed the side of the mountain before coming to a stop sideways in the road. The engine stalled. With no time to celebrate that he had kept his vehicle on top of the mountain, he slung off his seat belt, opened the console and palmed his Glock.

Car doors slammed. An engine roared to life. Headlights flashed on, blinding him. He flinched and lifted his hand to shield his eyes. There was no time to react before the impact of the vehicle jarred him. The gun flew from his hand and sailed across the dashboard, landing on the passenger side floorboard. Without the seat belt to hold him in place, Randy's shoulder slammed against the steering wheel. Then his body rebounded and his head smashed against the side window. Pain shot from his temple and exploded behind his eyes.

"No. No. No!" He pressed as hard as he could on the brake, trying to resist the force of the vehicle pushing his SUV toward the cliff. He struggled to get his bearings. If he could turn the wheels away from the cliff, he might make an escape. Twisting the steering wheel sharply to the right, he turned the key in the ignition. It sputtered, but didn't start. The sound of gravel crunched under his tires. They had reached the shoulder of the road. A few more feet and he'd be airborne. The pushing stopped. And the other vehicle backed up. Randy groped for the door handle. Before he could get free, his tormentors rammed into his SUV one last time, sending his vehicle careening over the side. Tree limbs broke and rocks pounded his vehicle as he tossed around inside like an old shoe in a washing machine.

The SUV flipped, and the door swung open.

Randy hurled through the air. He slammed against the side of the mountain, the muddy surface doing little to cushion the blow. Sliding down the rain-soaked mountain, he landed on a narrow ledge; the breath knocked out of him. Every inch of his body ached.

Car doors slammed overhead. Randy forced air into his lungs and pressed against the mountain. Wedging his body behind a small pine tree that was barely taller than his own six feet two inches, he prayed the men couldn't see him.

His SUV landed at the bottom of the ravine with a thud and exploded into a fiery ball. Heat and smoke engulfed Randy. He choked back a cough, anxious not to give away his hiding place.

"Looks like the world now has one less nosy cop," Torres laughed. "One down, one to go."

"You mean to tell me that not only did you lead him to me, but you haven't taken care of his partner yet?" a gravelly, masculine voice demanded.

The voice was very distinct, with a strong Southern accent that seemed out of place. Randy had the feeling he'd met the person speaking before, but he couldn't come up with the name that went with the voice.

"Boss, I promise, we have everything under control."

"No, you don't," the boss spat out, his disgust obvious. "That's why I'm here, to keep y'all from being arrested."

That voice. It sounded just like… No, it couldn't be. He shook his head and tried to focus on the discussion overhead. There'd be time to figure out who the boss was after Randy made it off the side of the mountain.

"As soon as we spotted the tail, I gave the order for Greg to take care of his partner."

The boss grunted. "Let's go. We're late for our meeting with my brother, and you need to call Greg to see if he got the girl."

No! Randy patted his pockets. He had to warn Katherine. Only, his phone was at the bottom of the ravine, being burned to a crisp.

The sound of vehicles leaving the scene echoed in the night. Randy used the pine tree for support and pushed to his feet, taking care not to put too much of his weight against the tree for fear its roots wouldn't be stable in the rain-soaked ground.

The ledge he stood on was maybe five feet wide, and the cliff was almost straight up. The light from the fire below illuminated the mountain enough that he could make out several rocks and grooves that could provide hand and foot holds. He was an experienced mountain climber, but he'd never climbed free solo on a mountain in a rainstorm. Or in the dark. The temperatures were falling. If he expected to get off this mountainside before hypothermia set in, he had no choice but to climb. Reaching for a rock that jutted out a few inches above his head, he started upward.

His bare hands were numb from the cold, wet rocks, but at the same time, the muscles in his arms felt like they were on fire. It seemed as if he'd been on the side of the mountain for hours. In reality, he knew it couldn't have been over fifteen minutes. If he focused on the discomfort his body was experiencing, he'd never make it to the top. And no one would find him until it was too late. *Focus.* Adrenaline spurred him on.

Finally, Randy pulled himself onto the gravel edge of the road. He'd made it. He rubbed his limbs, desperate to warm them and increase circulation.

Headlights came around the curve of the road. Were his tormentors returning?

A large boulder sat to his right. He crawled behind it and prayed it would provide enough cover to protect him until he determined if the approaching vehicle contained friend or foe.

A black four-door pickup truck came to a stop a couple of feet from his hiding place. A white-haired man with a beard stepped out of it and walked to the edge of the shoulder to peer over the cliff at the smoke.

Thank You, Lord. Help had arrived.

Randy pulled himself to his feet and slipped out from behind the boulder. "Thank you for stopping. I need—" A stabbing pain exploded in his left temple, then snaked behind his eye. His vision blurred, and a wave of nausea washed over him.

The man's face swirled before him. Randy squeezed his eyes shut. He had never experienced such an excruciating headache before. His body shook uncontrollably, whether from the pain or the cold, freezing rain he did not know. He stumbled, falling to his knees on the muddy ground. The man yelled for someone in the truck to call 911.

"Please, Lord, help me," Randy whispered.

You can't go to sleep. You hit your head. Stay awake, son. You might have a concussion. The childhood memory of his mom's urgent warning anytime he'd gotten a bump on the head echoed in his mind. Randy fought to stay awake, as she'd always advised, but the pain only intensified. *I'm sorry, Mom.* A blanket of total darkness engulfed him.

* * *

The sound of her heels clicking on the gray-and-blue ceramic tile floor echoed in the empty hallway as Agent Katherine Lewis made her way to the nurse's desk. When she'd received Randy's voice message, she'd hitched a ride to town with a teenage neighbor who worked as a pizza delivery guy. Then she'd rented a car and driven to the safe house in Laramie to await Randy's arrival. When he hadn't shown up, she had known something had gone terribly wrong.

Even though Randy—the lead on this investigation—had instructed her to do so, Katherine hadn't contacted Special Agent in Charge Wanda Richardson to apprise her of the situation. A long time ago, she had learned the importance of having all the facts in every situation. This was no different. She needed to know what went wrong and if they could salvage the investigation before reporting to Wanda.

So, Katherine had spent the past two days checking every morgue and hospital in a seventy-five-mile radius. Granted, the search would have been easier with the help of the Bureau, but she and Randy had invested too much time into busting the illegal horse racing ring, which would also take down a multistate drug ring. Blown cover or not, she wouldn't sacrifice their efforts by calling in backup. Not yet, anyway.

She took a deep breath and squared her shoulders. If she'd started her search in Colorado instead of limiting it to Wyoming in the beginning, she would have found the news story about the accident the night Randy disappeared sooner. The photo had shown an unrecognizable vehicle, but the article had said a medical transport helicopter took the victim to the hospital. The article hadn't listed the name of the hospital or given the condition of the victim, so she'd compiled a list of hospitals in the area and was currently visiting the second one on her list.

Katherine stepped up to the desk where an older woman with short gray hair typed on a laptop, a frown marring her face.

"Excuse me. Ma'am?"

"Yes?" the receptionist asked without glancing up.

Katherine removed her phone from the inner pocket of her suit jacket, pulled up a photo of Randy and laid the phone on the desk. "I'm looking for this man. He's been missing for several days. There's a good chance he was the driver of the burned vehicle that was pulled out of the canyon."

This seemed to catch the woman's attention. After a quick glance at the photo, she snatched the receiver off the desk phone and pressed a couple of numbers. "There's someone here asking about our John Doe."

"John Doe?" Katherine gripped the edge of the counter. They didn't know Randy's name, or at least the alias he would have used. Did this mean he was still unconscious? How critical were his injuries?

"Miss? Are you okay? You look pale." The woman stood and peered at her. "Do you need to sit down?"

"Um... No, I'm fine. Please, tell me is Age—" She swallowed the rest of the word and took a deep breath. She'd almost given his real name. *Don't blow it, Katherine. Protect your cover.*

"His name isn't John Doe. It's Mac. Harrison McGregor, that is. He's my...husband." Katherine always struggled to get that lie to cross her lips. The only part she hated about being a federal agent was the occasional necessary deception. Especially when it meant pretending to be someone's wife—a position she knew she'd never hold in real life. She hoped the nurse hadn't caught her near blunder. If so, maybe Katherine could play it off as the anxiety of a distraught *wife*.

The receptionist rounded the desk, sympathy in her dark eyes. "Mrs. McGregor, let's find you a quiet place to wait." She took Katherine's elbow and guided her down the hall to a small consultation room.

"I didn't mean to frighten you. Your husband is healthy and in good condition, considering…" She frowned and backed out the door. "The doctor will fill you in. I need to return to my desk."

Left alone with her thoughts, Katherine tried to decode the woman's words. *Healthy* and *in good condition* sounded promising. What had she meant by *considering*? *Considering*…he was in a coma? *Considering*…he was paralyzed? *Considering…*

The door opened, pulling Katherine from her thoughts. A tall blonde woman with a stethoscope draped around her neck entered the small space. "Mrs. McGregor, I'm Dr. Leah Barrett. And this," she added, stepping aside to reveal a white-haired man with a beard, "is Sheriff Grant Walker."

"Ma'am," he greeted her with a slight nod.

Katherine stood and pulled herself to her full five-foot-nine-inch height. "Dr. Barrett, what is this all about? How is my husband?"

"Ma'am, before Dr. Barrett can disclose any information, we need some proof the man in question is indeed your husband." The sheriff pierced her with a stern gaze. "HIPAA laws. I'm sure you understand."

"I'm not sure what kind of proof you're looking for, Sheriff. Other than some photos and my ID, I don't know what I can show you." She fidgeted with the slender gold band she'd slipped onto her left ring finger one month ago when this undercover-marriage assignment began. Prior to that time, she'd been the silent partner, doing the legwork and digging for clues behind the scenes.

Dr. Barrett took her arm and led her to a chair. "Please sit. We'll get this all sorted out quickly, and then I'll take you to your husband."

Katherine didn't miss the look that shot between the doctor and the sheriff. It seemed they weren't in total agreement on how to handle things. Good. Maybe she could appeal to the doctor's compassionate side, her sense of love and family, and sway her to let Katherine see Randy.

She pulled her phone back out and showed them the three pictures she had of Randy. One photo where Randy was driving, and she had taken a selfie with him in the background. Another where he leaned against a fence post and gave her a bored look. And finally, the one of them together that was their fake wedding photo. Katherine held a small bouquet and wore a simple white Sunday dress, and Randy wore a dark blue suit. All taken at the insistence of SAC Richardson when she decided the best way to get eyes and ears in Torres's private space was for Katherine to apply for a part-time housekeeping position. With Randy already working as a ranch hand, Wanda had thought having them pose as a married couple would keep them from looking suspicious if someone caught them talking on premises or riding together to and from work.

"How badly is Mac hurt? Why didn't someone call me and tell me he was here? My name and number are listed as his in-case-of-emergency contact in his cell phone."

"We could ask you the same thing. Why didn't you call or come by sooner? Or at the least, why didn't you file a missing person's report? What are you hiding?" Sheriff Walker shot one question after the other in rapid succession.

"If you must know, Mac and I got into an argument right before he left home on his business trip. When he didn't call to let me know he'd arrived safely, I figured he was still angry. So I gave him a day to cool off. It wasn't until yesterday that I got really worried after not being able to reach him. Then I saw the news report of the vehicle that crashed and burned, and—" More lies. At least she'd had enough sense to practice this tale beforehand; however, it hadn't kept her voice from cracking. She hoped the added emotion helped her case, although the look on the sheriff's face wasn't totally reassuring. "If I didn't locate him today, I had planned on filing a missing person's report.

"Look, you can think I'm a horrible wife if you want, but we've only been married a few months. We're still learning each other's little idiosyncrasies. I truly care about Mac and need him to be okay." This was accurate enough. If they were going to take down the drug crime ring, she needed him well and on top of his game.

Sheriff Walker raised an eyebrow but remained silent.

Katherine rarely took an instant disliking to anyone, but she was feeling very annoyed by the lawman. Why was he here anyway? Before she could voice the question, Dr. Barrett cleared her throat, pulling Katherine's attention back to her.

"Mrs. McGregor, we couldn't call you. When they brought your husband into the ER, he didn't have a cell phone or identification. We assume he lost those items when the vehicle exploded. The best we can tell, your husband wasn't wearing a seat belt when his vehicle went off the side of the mountain. He was thrown from the vehicle, which in this case probably saved his life. He suffered cracked ribs and a concussion."

Relief washed over Katherine. Randy was okay. He'd need time to recover, but they wouldn't have to abandon their mission. "Can I see him, please?"

Dr. Barrett looked at the sheriff as if seeking his approval. He shrugged. "If you ladies will excuse me, I'll get going."

Turning to her, he added, "Mrs. McGregor, I need information for the accident report. I'm sure you won't mind stopping by the station when you leave the hospital, right?" He tilted his hat and strolled out the door, not waiting on a reply. Did his response mean he believed her story? Maybe she was a better actress than she thought. Or maybe he was waiting to get her alone to grill her.

"Before I take you to see your husband, you need to know he was unconscious when he arrived," Dr. Barrett said solemnly. "Then we had to sedate him to manage his pain, keeping him in a semiconscious state. It wasn't until this morning that he was actually alert enough to talk to us."

"And?" Katherine wished the doctor would get to the point.

"He has amnesia."

An involuntary gasp escaped her lips. After seeing the photos of Randy's vehicle, a thousand "what-ifs" had wandered through Katherine's mind, but in all the scenarios, she'd never once imagined amnesia. Wasn't that something that only happened in the movies or old spy novels?

"I believe it's temporary," Dr. Barrett rushed on. "None of his scans show anything that would indicate permanent memory loss. We'll keep him here a few days and monitor him, but there's a good chance his memory won't return until he's back home, in familiar surroundings."

Katherine's mind whirled as the doctor escorted her to the room where the man she'd known for almost a year would look at her as a stranger. What was she going to do now? How could she help him recover his memory without compromising the investigation? She didn't have the answers, but Katherine would do whatever was necessary to stay on this case and save another family from the heartache her family had suffered when they'd lost her older brother to a drug addiction.

"This is his room," Dr. Barrett declared, pulling Katherine back to the present.

The doctor held the door and motioned for her to enter. Rich laughter echoed in the room as Randy sat up in bed watching an old black-and-white movie. Katherine wasn't sure what she had expected to see, but it wasn't the scene before her.

"It looks like our patient is feeling better," Dr. Barrett said warmly.

"Oh, hiya, Doc. Yeah, the meds helped my headache…" Randy's words faded as his eyes locked on Katherine. His brow furrowed.

"I brought you a visitor. This is—"

"Erin?"

A smile spread across her face, and her heart soared. He knew her alias and had sense enough to protect their cover in front of the doctor.

She moved to his bedside. "Hi, Mac. I'm sorry it took me so long to get here."

"Mac. My name is Mac. And you're Erin." He searched her face. "You're really real? I thought you were just a dream brought on by the sedatives." He turned to the doctor, a smile splitting his face. "My memories are returning. This is my wife. Isn't she beautiful? The thing I remember most is how her smile can brighten the darkest day."

His words hit Katherine like a kick to the gut. Something was off. Randy would never call her beautiful. He believed in keeping things on a business level, even when undercover. He would have simply said she was his wife, maybe added they were newlyweds, but nothing gushy.

She placed her hand on his shoulder and looked into his eyes for any signs her partner was acting. "Tell me about the accident. What happened?"

"The doc said my vehicle went off the side of a mountain during a thunderstorm." He frowned "Where was I headed in such a bad storm?"

Afraid of giving away too much in front of the doctor, Katherine chose her words carefully. "You were following our *employer* to a business meeting. Could he have seen the accident? Was there another vehicle involved?"

"I don't remember." He shook his head, confusion evident on his face. "I can't—"

"Mrs. McGregor, I must ask you to stop with all the questions," the doctor interrupted, reproach in her voice. "I know you want answers, but interrogating your husband isn't going to help him remember any faster."

There were a dozen questions she still needed answered. Had the rainstorm really caused the accident? Or had Torres spotted Randy tailing him and forced his vehicle off the road? A sinking feeling settled in her stomach. Randy was one of the safest drivers she had ever known. It was unlikely the accident had been driver error. Which left her with one more question. Had Torres figured out they were undercover agents?

She met the doctor's gaze and nodded. Katherine would save the rest of her unanswered questions for later. At least the most important one had been answered.

Randy's memories hadn't returned—Mac's had.

TWO

The pain hit suddenly and fiercely, exploding behind his eyes and spreading to his temples. Mac winced and clutched his head, falling back against the pillow. Squeezing his eyelids closed, he pressed his palms against his temples and desperately tried to push the pain away.

Movement swarmed around him, footsteps running, a door opening and closing…every sound amplified by a thousand. Then, soft hands covered his as if trying to help cradle his head. He opened his eyes and found Erin watching him. A frown creased her brow.

How was it he could remember her face and name, but the rest of his memory—his childhood, his career, meeting her, their wedding, their life together—was a jumbled, cloudy mess?

Dr. Barrett rushed back into the room, a syringe in her hand and a nurse close behind.

"We're going to give you something to ease the headache. What you're experiencing is a migraine brought on by a combination of the concussion and the stress of trying to regain your memory."

He dropped his hands and caught one of Erin's, gripping it tightly. A memory flashed in his mind's eye. *A small child was about to get a shot, and he was screaming and flailing around. There was a woman—his mom?— struggling to hold the boy as the doctor came closer. She put her hands on either side of his face, turning him so he'd look at her.* Mac was the child. He caught his breath, and the memory vanished as quickly as it had arrived.

Mac may not have his full memory, but he knew he wouldn't want to seem squeamish in front of his wife. He closed his eyes and pushed air through clenched teeth as the doctor administered the meds. A few minutes and several slow, deep breaths later, the pain subsided, becoming more of a dull ache.

He looked up at Erin. "Thank you for finding me."

"Of course. I've got your six."

"Six? What does that mean?"

"It means I've got your back. We're partners. We look out for each other." A strange look crossed her eyes briefly before she looked away, as if trying to shelter him from some unknown truth.

What was she hiding from him?

A wave of sleepiness washed over him, and he faintly heard Dr. Barrett telling Erin that the meds she'd administered contained a sedative that would help him rest. No! Mac struggled to remain awake and focused...like he had the other night, outside, in the icy rain. Where had that thought come from? Was it a memory from his accident? Or was it an older memory from some other time? If only he could think clearly.

He needed to talk to Erin and fill the gaps in his memory. Why was he in the hospital? And why didn't he remember anything prior to their marriage?

"Are you sure it's just a migraine and not something more serious from his head injury?" Erin asked in a hushed whisper.

"Mrs. McGregor, I assure you we've run all the tests and scans. This is perfectly normal considering his concussion and memory loss," Dr. Barrett replied in an authoritative yet calming manner. "Now, I must get on with my rounds. If you need anything, press the call button and a nurse will assist you. I'll check back in on your husband in a few hours. In the meantime, sleep is the best medicine for his body, and mind, to heal completely."

Mac struggled to remain alert, fighting his weighted eyelids. The more he fought, the more his energy drained. He lacked the strength to fight his body's desire for sleep.

Just as he gave in to the heaviness of his eyelids and allowed them to close, he heard the scraping sound of a chair being pulled close to his bedside and felt Erin's gentle touch as her hand covered his. Warmth radiated up his arm, comforting him. He flipped his hand over and laced his fingers around hers. His wife wasn't going anywhere. He'd get answers after the fog engulfing him lifted.

Katherine placed her free hand firmly on her knee, forcing it to stop bouncing. She'd tried for years to break her fidgeting habit, but to no avail, especially when she struggled to make a decision. Should she call SAC Richardson? Or wait until she had more facts and a better understanding of the situation?

What time was it? She craned her neck to look at the wristwatch on Randy's arm. The acrylic crystal that covered the face was cracked and the hands had stopped moving. She sighed. Her partner would be upset when he regained his memory and realized his cherished possession had been damaged in the accident. Twisting in her chair she located a clock on the wall behind her. Randy had been sleeping for almost four hours. She hoped he'd wake up minus the migraine and with his full memory restored, but most of all she hoped he'd wake up soon. Her hand was hot and sweaty. Every time she tried to slip it out of his grasp, his grip tightened.

Examining his face, she noted the bruises. There was a nasty-looking mark punctuated by a line of stitches that ran from his temple to his cheek. Was that the blow that had triggered his memory loss? She lifted her hand, her finger an inch from his face, before she realized what she was doing. Closing her hand, her fingernails digging into her palm, she let it drop onto her lap. If his memories didn't return when he woke up, she'd have to tell him the truth. They were coworkers, not husband and wife. They barely knew each other in spite of the fact that they'd lived together in the same house for the past three months, coexisting as roommates who randomly had meals together but never shared any deep dark secrets.

She needed to escape, just for a moment, so she could clear her head and think about their next plan of action. Mainly how to get Randy out of the hospital and to the safe house without Torres's goons finding them.

Maybe if she stopped trying to be subtle about it and quickly pulled away like a magician jerking a tablecloth off a table set with fine china, she'd free her hand without waking Randy. One. Two. Three. She pulled away. Randy moaned in protest, grabbed a fistful of the blanket and smiled, never waking.

Katherine released a breath and slowly eased her way out of the hard chair she'd been sitting in. As soon as she stood, a pins-and-needles type of pain pierced the bottoms of her feet. She gritted her teeth to keep from crying out. Taking tentative steps, she tried to get the blood flowing again.

A nurse entered the room. "Good evening, Mrs. McGregor. My name's Samantha. I'm the night-shift nurse." She crossed to the bed and replaced the bag of IV fluids before checking Randy's blood pressure, pulse and oxygen levels. "Everything looks good. Hopefully you can get this handsome man of yours out of here soon."

"Any idea of how soon?" Katherine asked. "I know that decision is up to the doctors, but do you have any guesses when they'll release my, um, Mac?"

"Oh, I'd say you might be out of here as

early as tomorrow." The nurse nodded toward the bed. "The cracked ribs and bruising can heal at home."

"What about his amnesia?"

"Amnesia doesn't require hospitalization for treatment. It just takes time." The nurse smiled and headed to the door, where she paused and looked back at her. "Love and faith are the best medicines for most ailments, including amnesia. Love your husband. Be patient with him when he struggles to remember. Above all else, pray and have faith that the Lord will restore his memories."

Pray and have faith.

Katherine couldn't remember the last time she had a conversation with God. She truly hoped Randy's recovery didn't rest on her ability to pray and have faith.

Where was he? He couldn't get his bearings. The room was dark, except for a sliver of light that peeked under the door and an eerie green glow from some type of monitor to his left. What would happen if he touched it? Would it sound an alarm? He lifted his arm, and that's when he noticed the needle in the back of his hand. An IV? He was in the hospital. The memories of the day came flooding back to him.

"Erin…" The name came out as a strangled whisper. He licked his lips. His throat was as dry as a blistering summer day in the Mojave Desert.

How did he know that? Had he ever been to the Mojave Desert? More questions that he hoped Erin could help him answer. Mac turned his head, searching for her. After a few moments, his eyes adjusted to the darkness, and he could make out her silhouette curled up in the chair a few feet from his bedside.

The panic that had threatened to overtake him subsided at the sight of her. He might not have many memories, but he sensed that as long as they were together everything would be alright.

He rolled to his side and winced. "Ow." In his desire to have a better view of her, he'd forgotten his cracked ribs.

Her eyelids flew open, and she bounded out of the chair. "Are you okay? Do you need the nurse?"

She leaned over him, searching his eyes, her face mere inches above his. A strand of her long brown hair fell like a shield between them, and he caught a whiff of her citrus-scented shampoo. Mac reached out and tucked the hair behind her ear. Erin startled slightly but didn't pull back, her eyes never leaving his.

Burying his fingers in her hair, he cupped the back of her head and pulled her face close. His lips touched hers for the briefest second before she pulled away. Not the kiss he'd hoped for, but still nice, although it ended way too soon.

Erin stepped back from his bedside, her hand against her lips. Why had she pulled away from his kiss? And why did she have a look of shock on her face? They were married. They'd kissed before.

"I can...it seems...you're fine," she stammered. "Um... How's the headache? Do you need me to buzz the nurse?"

He braced his forearm on the mattress and pushed upward. A stabbing pain shot through his lungs. Catching his breath, he collapsed against the mattress and wrapped his arms tightly around his middle.

Erin found the cable that dangled from the bed rail and pressed the call button attached to the end, all the while telling him to "breathe, slow and steady breaths."

How was he supposed to do that when every time his lungs expanded or contracted burning pain radiated in his chest?

Mac puffed air through clenched teeth, wishing he had stopped her from buzzing the nurse. He was desperate for the pain to subside, but he'd prefer not to have additional meds pumped into his body. If the darkness peeping through the blinds was any indication, he'd already slept the day away, and he had no desire to fall back into a drug-induced slumber.

"Can I help you?" A female voice sounded over the intercom system.

"Yes. Ra—Mac is awake and in pain. Please, can you give him something?"

The unknown voice said she'd review his chart to see what the doctor had ordered, and then she'd be in to check on him.

His wife ordered the nurse to be fast and gave him a forced smile. Erin had fire in her eyes. It seemed he'd married a fighter, someone who looked after the people she cared about.

Mac bit back the laugh that tickled his throat, sensing not only would she not appreciate it but also laughing would only incite more pain.

He touched her hand that rested on the bed rail. "It's okay. I'm fine. I forgot about the cracked ribs and moved too quickly. Could you please press the button to raise the head of the bed?"

Just as he got settled into a semi-upright position, the nurse entered, carrying a tray with a cup of water and a small paper medicine cup.

"Dr. Barrett has prescribed an anti-inflammatory." She tipped two pills into the palm of his hand.

"Will these make me sleepy?"

"No. They shouldn't."

After he'd downed the pills, the nurse picked up the volumetric exerciser that sat on the tray table and handed it to him. "Time to exercise your lungs. We don't want you to get pneumonia."

He accepted the small plastic breathing device and glanced over at Erin, who stood at the window with her back to the room. Even from the side view, he could tell something troubled her. Why had the kiss disturbed her so deeply? What was his wife not telling him?

Katherine gazed out the window at the bright full moon in the night sky. She never should have leaned over Randy. She had wanted to see if he recognized her as Katherine, not Erin. Guess she got her answer.

Wrapping her arms around her stomach, she tried to calm the quivering tremble that had started the instant his lips touched hers. Nervous energy coursed through her body, her heart pounding in her chest like a caged hummingbird. The last time she had felt this kind of adrenaline rush was her thirteenth birthday, after stepping off the Flying Dragon roller coaster. A ride she had only ridden to keep her friends from making fun of her for being afraid. Katherine had never been a thrill seeker, not at age thirteen and definitely not at age thirty-six. Another reason she had tried to keep things strictly professional between her and Randy.

Katherine had spent her years alone by choice, dedicating all of her time to her career. There wasn't room for romance in her life. The instant she met Agent Randy Ingalls, she knew this assignment would be her most challenging. Aunt Mae had taught her long ago that while most women worried about their future husband getting the four Cs of a diamond right, it was far more important to worry about the four Cs of a quality husband. And Randy Ingalls was the only man that she'd met to fit all four qualities…captivating, confident, caring and cute.

Absentmindedly touching her lips, she mentally berated herself for letting her guard down and allowing Randy to get close enough to kiss her. After Nelson ended their engagement—saying two agents as dedicated to their careers as they were would never be able to make a marriage work—she had promised herself she'd never date a coworker again. Of course,

Katherine could only be mad at herself for the brief kiss and not Randy. He thought they were married.

Her face warmed, and she leaned against the cool glass of the window. That's when she saw them. Two men wearing caps pulled low over their faces stepped out of the shadow of the emergency room entryway. She couldn't make out their faces. The shorter one pointed in her direction, motioned for the other guy to follow and took off running into the hospital.

The room they were in was on the second floor of the small hospital. It wouldn't take long for the men to reach them.

Moving back to Randy's bedside, she addressed the nurse. "If you have other work to attend to, I can watch him do the breathing exercises."

"That'd be great." The nurse smiled and left.

No sooner had the door closed than Katherine bolted across the room and searched the small wardrobe, opening the large door and then all the drawers. Empty. She turned back to Randy and demanded, "Where are your clothes?"

Opening his mouth and dropping the mouthpiece, he coughed out the breath he'd been inhaling. "What?"

"Clothes. Where are they?"

"I'm not sure. Maybe we could ask the nurse." He reached for the call button.

"No!" she whisper-screamed.

Time was running out. She rushed to the door, cracked it open and peeked out just as the two men stepped off the elevator at the other end of the hall. They were still too far away to identify, but she knew they were after her and Randy.

She closed the door and hurried to his bedside. "No time to explain. We've got to move. Fast. And we've got to be quiet. Our lives depend on it."

Randy looked as if he were going to argue, but thought better of it and nodded. Then he gritted his teeth and jerked the IV needle out of his arm. He gestured for her to unplug the vital signs monitor, and then he disentangled himself from all the wires and reached over to power off the monitor before the battery backup could set off the alarm. How did he know to do that? With no time to ponder the answer, she watched in awe as he took a deep breath and stood, confident and strong.

Was his training so ingrained into his mind to where he could function on autopilot, even without his memories? Katherine sure hoped so.

Her mind raced as she ran different scenarios through it, trying to hit on an idea that would help them make their escape. Randy stood before her, pain etched on his face, ready to do whatever she asked of him.

Ugh. She should have already had an exit plan in place for an emergency like this. Instead, she'd spent the last few hours trying to process the fact that Randy thought he was Mac and she was his wife. In the ten years that she'd been an agent, she never dreamed of a situation like this. Now she had to think fast, or they'd both be dead.

THREE

The voices in the hall grew louder. Katherine only caught bits and pieces of the words, but it seemed one man was trying to convince the nurse he was Randy's brother.

She met Randy's gaze and put her index finger to her lips, indicating he should stay quiet. Then she crossed to the door, inched it open and peeked around it. The nurse was trying to get the men to leave, telling them it was past visiting hours, and she'd have the patient or family member call them the next day. Their backs were to Katherine, but they squared their shoulders in an obvious attempt to posture their position. They wouldn't be going anywhere.

She couldn't get both her and Randy out of the room without attracting attention, and she wasn't about to leave him behind in the hospital. Maybe she could create the illusion they had both escaped. It would be risky, but what other option did she have that wouldn't result in a possible shootout inside the hospital?

Hurrying back toward Randy, she motioned for him to follow her into the bathroom. She'd noticed a shower in there earlier. Not the best hiding place, but it would have to do. To Randy's credit, he stayed on her heels and didn't make a sound, even though she knew he had to be in excruciating pain. Cracked ribs were no joke.

Katherine pulled back the dark blue shower curtain and turned to allow Randy to enter the small space ahead of her, accidentally elbowing him in the ribs. He grimaced and pressed his lips together. She mouthed "I'm sorry," and he rewarded her with a half smile as he stepped past her into the shower.

She leaned in close and whispered, "I promise to explain all this to you once we get some place safe. For now, please, no matter what happens, stay quiet and don't move. I'll be right back."

Before he could reply, she stepped back into the room and headed toward the door. Time to check and see if the two goons were still harassing the night-duty nurse. Or if she had gotten them to leave.

Raised voices in the hallway warned her the nurse hadn't been able to control the two men.

"That's it! I'm calling security," the nurse declared in a wobbly, not-so-stern voice. There was a clattering noise. "Unhand me!"

Katherine palmed her service revolver. Although she'd really hate to answer all the questions involved if she discharged a round inside a hospital, like it or not, she may have no choice but to use her weapon to stop these men from killing someone.

Taking a deep breath, she puffed the air out and poked her head around the door. Greg, Torres's right-hand man, held the nurse with an arm wrapped completely around her small body, her arms pinned to her side. The nurse, who looked to be in her early thirties, flailed around, demanding to be let go. Greg pulled a gun out of the waistband of his jeans and held it beside her temple, the barrel pointed toward the ceiling. At least he wasn't looking to kill an innocent person, only to scare her. For now.

Greg nodded to the other guy, a lanky, dark-haired man she'd never seen before. "Start checking all the rooms until you find them." He tightened his grip on the nurse, and she cried out in pain. "I'll control her. Now, move!"

The dark-haired man was on the other end of the hall. Katherine had to act fast. She quickly scanned the hospital floor map taped onto the back of the door. Stairs were on either end of the hall, with the closest ones to the right, two doors away. The plan forming in her head wasn't one she really loved. Like most plans involving criminals, it wasn't foolproof. But she didn't have any other options. With no time to analyze every scenario, she had to trust her gut. Something she'd battled to do for many years. She would not let Randy down, even if it meant leaving him behind while she tried to lead the gunmen away from the area.

Please, Lord, let them follow me. Don't let them harm anyone else. The prayer came naturally and unbidden, even though she'd lived most of her adult life since she'd last prayed. Had the nurse's comment earlier planted the idea of praying in her head? Would God even recognize her voice and her need? No time to worry about that. Besides, she could take care of herself and everyone around her, just like she always did.

One last glance down the hall showed the dark-haired man disappearing into a room five doors away and the nurse still putting up a fight, which was keeping Greg distracted. Katherine didn't know where any of the other nurses or orderlies might be. Being the night shift, it wouldn't be uncommon for the hospital to be staffed with a smaller crew. Maybe the rest of the staff were on a dinner break, or perhaps they heard the commotion and were hiding. Katherine couldn't blame them if they were.

Okay. Time to go. She eased the door open wide enough to show the empty room and give the appearance that they had escaped and released a quiet sigh of thanksgiving that the door hadn't squeaked.

Her back to the wall, she hurried to the stairwell, keeping constant watch over her shoulder. Once she made it to her destination, she opened the door and waited for one of the men to see her.

The dark-haired man stepped back into the hall and started toward the next room, his steps faltering when he spotted her. "Hey!" He stood frozen in place, almost as if he couldn't believe his eyes.

"Grab her!" Greg released the nurse and shoved her out of his way.

Pretending to speak to someone in the stairwell, Katherine yelled, "Go! Get out of here, Mac. I'll hold them off."

One more quick look into the hallway showed both men bearing down on her and the nurse backing into a patient's room with a cell phone to her ear. Hopefully, she was calling security. Katherine could definitely do with some backup right about now.

She stepped onto the stairwell landing and pulled the heavy metal door closed, then quickly slipped out of her heels and wedged one into the lever door handle. If it worked the way she hoped, the two goons wouldn't be able to get into the stairwell without going to another floor to access it. And if her shoe trick failed, maybe it would at least slow them down a bit and she could stay a few steps ahead of them until help arrived.

Up or down? Which way would they expect her to go? Down. To exit the building. Okay, up it was.

Time to call her boss and request an agent to come in and extract them. Bolting up the stairs, she reached into her back pocket. Her cell phone wasn't there. Ugh. She must have dropped it in Randy's room. Okay, so they'd be on their own for a little longer. No worries. Yeah, right.

Greg and his friend were working hard to get the door open. Her shoe wouldn't hold much longer. Picking up the pace, she pushed upward. She needed to be out of sight before they entered the dimly lit stairwell to keep from giving away her location.

The sound of someone hitting the metal door echoed in the stairwell, blending with the sound of her feet pounding on each step as she ascended to who knew what. More of Torres's men or, hopefully, police backup?

The first-floor door banged open, and she pressed against the wall, praying they wouldn't see her. She heard diminishing footsteps as the person descended downward to the underground parking deck. Holding her breath, she eased up the last two steps to the next floor's landing and inched the door open. At almost the same instant, the heel on the shoe she'd jammed into the door handle broke, and Greg stumbled onto the landing below. Their eyes met briefly before she catapulted through the fourth-floor door and raced down the hall.

What was he doing? Mac might not have all his memories, but he didn't believe he was the type of person to hide in the shower. He pulled back the curtain and started across the tiny bathroom. His foot connected with a small object, sending it skittering across the floor. It came to a stop next to the toilet. Holding his breath, he grasped the metal handrail and bent to retrieve the item. It was a cell phone. Erin must have dropped it.

His hospital room was empty. Where had his wife gone? What had startled her?

He crept over to the door and peered out as a man disappeared into the stairwell. A security guard and an orderly charged down the hall from the opposite end, while one of the nurses frantically explained that two men with guns were chasing an amnesia patient and his wife. They were talking about him and Erin.

Mac needed to find her. Now. And protect her from whatever danger they were facing. He started out of the room and stopped midstride. The nurse, orderly and guard were headed his way. If they saw him, they'd force him back to bed and press him for answers he didn't have. Stepping into the shadow behind the door, he held his breath as the trio charged past his room. He needed to find Erin.

Slipping into the hall, he headed the opposite direction from the trio, acutely aware he wouldn't get far in his hospital gown.

On the other side of the nurses' station was a small room with a door that said Hospital Personnel Only. Mac hurried over, mildly surprised when he turned the knob and the door opened. He glanced over his shoulder to make sure no one was around before stepping into the room that appeared to be a lounge area. Cabinets that housed a microwave, coffeepot, sink and refrigerator lined one wall, and in the center of the room there was a wooden dinette table and chairs. A row of lockers ran along the back wall with a door on either side of them, one labeled Women and the other Men.

The lockers, with miniature chalkboard-style nameplates identifying the owner of the contents, had built-in combination locks. That wouldn't stop Mac from trying to open them. Perhaps he would find someone as lazy as Steve, his high school best friend who would close his lock to make it appear locked but wouldn't actually spin the dial, thus avoiding the hassle of having to rework the code every time. His hand froze midair as he reached for the first lock. Where had that thought come from? Hope surged within him. Maybe his memories were returning. He'd have to analyze this random memory later. For now, he had to find clothes, then locate Erin.

Bam. The fourth lock he tried popped right open. He peered at the name of the owner. Joe. The orderly who had helped him that morning. He'd been about the same height as Mac, but he'd appeared to be a size or two larger in clothing.

Please, Lord, let there be something in this locker that I can wear out of here. I need to find my wife before someone hurts her.

The metal door squeaked as he opened it, and he winced. He needed to hurry. He found a pair of gray sweats. Yep. Size XL. They'd be baggy on him, but they had a drawstring tie inside the waistband, so they'd do. Looking deeper into the locker, he also discovered a green-and-gold Colorado State hoodie and a pair of sneakers only a half size too small for him. He'd make it work.

Mac quickly changed out of his standard-issue patient gown and into the borrowed clothes. He couldn't think of himself as a thief. Closing the locker, he muttered, "I'll return your clothes as soon as I can, Joe. I promise."

Time to move.

Peering out into the hall, he saw several patients huddled together on the opposite end near the stairs. Hospital staff members were trying to get everyone to return to their rooms. The elevator pinged. The doors opened and a police officer stepped out. A man of law without a nurse or orderly by his side. Mac's heart lifted. Maybe he could appeal to the officer's sense of duty and family and could work with the man to locate Erin before the two men with guns did.

Mac was about to step out of the staff lounge when movement caught his attention. Erin came around the corner and put out her hand to stop the elevator doors from closing. She met his gaze and gave a stern shake of her head, motioning for him to follow her. He darted out of the staff lounge and raced past the officer and into the elevator.

"Hey, you. Stop!" The officer lunged to stop the heavy doors from closing, but he wasn't fast enough. They closed inches in front of his outstretched hand.

Mac sucked in air through clenched teeth as piercing pain gripped his chest. Leaning against the back wall of the elevator, he fought to overcome the wave of nausea that threatened. He really had to stop making sudden moves.

"Are you okay?" Erin asked over her shoulder as she stood with one index finger firmly pressed against the Close Door button and her other index finger pressed against the button for the basement level.

"I'm fine." He puffed out one more breath and pushed to a stand. "What are you doing?"

After the elevator jolted and started its descent, she dropped her hands and turned to face him with a shrug. "It's a trick to keep the elevator from stopping on any other floors but the one you're going to. Press and hold both buttons until the elevator moves, and voilà."

His wife was full of surprises. He'd like to question her further and discover her other hidden talents. But for now, he needed to find out what was going on and figure a way out of the situation they were in.

"So, can you tell me about the men after us?"

"I'll answer your questions once we're someplace safe."

"And how are we going to ditch those guys and the police and—wait a minute. Why are we running from the police? Are we criminals?"

Green flecks sparkled in her blue eyes, and her jaw dropped, her shocked surprise evident. Relief washed over him. "Okay, so we're not criminals."

"Um…no." The elevator dinged, signaling their arrival in the basement. She motioned for him to hang back. "Let me go first."

The doors opened. A gun appeared in her hand, and she stepped out of the elevator into the underground parking garage. After a quick look around, she motioned for him to follow her. "Stay close. If we can make it to my rental car, we'll go to the safe house and call Wanda to send someone to extract us from this situation."

His mind raced. What kind of people required extraction? He stopped short. Spies?

"We're not spies," Erin said without even looking backward.

A smile sprang to his lips. Their marriage must be a strong one if she could read his mind.

A black, late-model four-door pickup truck came to a stop in front of them. The passenger side window rolled down, and a white-haired man demanded they get in. Erin stepped back, doubt on her face.

"Wanda sent me. Get in, now!" the man demanded.

A dark-colored Jeep with a crushed fender screeched around the corner, barreling in their direction. This spurred Erin into action. She pulled open the back door of the pickup truck and pushed Mac in ahead of her. Then she scrambled in and slammed the door behind her. "Go, go, go!"

Mac didn't know who any of these people were, not their driver, or the men chasing them, or the mysterious Wanda. The only person he knew and trusted was Erin, but even that trust was in jeopardy at the moment. What kind of nightmare had he woken up to?

FOUR

Katherine had to give the sheriff credit. When she yelled "go," he floored the gas. They zoomed between the rows of parked cars. She glanced back as they rounded the corner toward the exit. Their pursuers were drawing nearer when a light blue Volkswagen Beetle started backing out of a parking spot right in front of them. Sheriff Walker swerved and sped around the Beetle, barely escaping a collision. The driver of the Jeep attempted to mimic the sheriff's maneuver but didn't have enough clearance. The sound of metal scraping against metal echoed like fingernails on a chalkboard. Horns blew and yelling ensued.

Whew. That was close. She settled into her seat just as the sheriff pulled up to the gate and tossed coins into the machine. The barrier lifted, and they pulled out into the night.

"Are you ready to tell me what's going on?"

Randy asked calmly, tilting his head toward the front seat. "And who, exactly, is our driver?"

Sheriff Walker's raised eyebrow met her gaze in the rearview mirror. "Do you mean to tell me he really does have amnesia?"

Only able to answer one question at a time, she started with the easy one. "Our driver is Sheriff Grant Walker. I met him when I arrived at the hospital." She turned to the man in the front seat. "Why didn't you tell me you knew Wanda?"

"Because I didn't know there was a connection. Not then anyway." He merged onto the interstate. "I simply used my contacts to do a little digging. To find out your...*identities*."

He knew their identities. Agents working undercover as a married couple. "So, you know everything?"

"Not everything, but enough. Look, it's just over an hour's drive to my hunting cabin. I'll fill you in on my conversation with Wanda. But first, I need to call the station and put out an APB for the Jeep."

That sounded reasonable enough. Deal with the immediate risk first and then hash out the details. She couldn't really argue with him. After all, she had been putting Randy off all day, telling him she would clue him in when they got to a safer location.

The sheriff called dispatch, and Katherine turned her attention to her injured partner. "Are you okay? You're not hurt from the mad dash out of the hospital, are you?"

"No. I'm fine. Just trying to put all the puzzle pieces together in my head." He gave her a half smile.

"What have you figured out so far?"

Was she being a coward, hoping he could put most of the events together? Wasn't it best if his lost memories returned without her forcing the information into place? Probably, yes, on both counts. But in all fairness, this wasn't a normal situation.

"You said we aren't criminals." He leaned in and continued in hushed tones, "And we're not spies. So, the only conclusion I can come up with is that we're in witness protection. We must have found out something really dangerous about the men who are chasing us." He pulled back and searched her eyes. "Am I right?"

"Looks like they found us. Fasten your seat belts and hang on tight," the sheriff commanded before she could respond to Randy's question.

The Jeep raced up behind them. Sheriff Walker sped up, keeping as much distance as possible between them as he talked to dispatch and requested immediate backup.

Being the middle of the night, the interstate was practically deserted. The only other vehicle in sight was at least a mile ahead of them. Katherine palmed her service revolver.

"What are you planning to do?" Randy asked.

"Buy us some time until backup gets here." She met the sheriff's gaze in the rearview mirror, and he nodded consent.

"Let me." Randy held out his palm. "If my memory is correct, I'm a pretty good sharpshooter."

"Normally, you're one of the best, but we can't take that chance today. Not when you're recovering from a head wound." She met his gaze. "I've got it. This time."

Gathering her hair into a ponytail, she secured it into place with the elastic hair tie she wore around her wrist. She rolled down the window, then climbed into the front passenger seat and rolled down that window as well.

"Don't shoot to kill. Just try to keep them at bay until help arrives," Sheriff Walker ordered. "We need them alive to know why they're after you."

"Got it." She took a deep breath and exhaled the tension building inside her.

"Mac, get down on the floor in case they return fire," she commanded. Not waiting to see if he followed her orders, she shoved the upper half of her body through the opening and twisted to sit on the window frame. Then she thrust her left hand through the opening of the back window and hooked her arm around the doorframe for support.

Arms wrapped around her legs in a viselike grip, and she stiffened. "What..."

"I'll keep you from falling," Randy shouted gruffly. "I may have amnesia, but I'm not a child. And I'm not helpless." From this angle she couldn't see him, but a warm sensation engulfed her despite the cold wind lashing at her upper body. Amnesia or not, her partner still had her back.

Before she could say anything, the Jeep changed lanes and charged toward her. No time to argue. She aimed and shot three rounds in rapid succession into the grille of the vehicle. Smoke billowed out. The Jeep started slowing and fell back behind the sheriff's truck. A rifle appeared out of the passenger side window of the Jeep and Katherine slid back inside the truck, ducking low in the seat as the bullet hit the back window.

To her amazement, it didn't shatter. "You have bulletproof glass in your personal vehicle?"

"My brother-in-law owns an auto body

shop." Sheriff Walker shrugged. "The glass is more bullet resistant than bulletproof. It may stop one or two bullets, but it won't stop a barrage of gunfire." He accelerated, and the distance between them widened.

The Jeep's engine was really smoking now. The vehicle slowed. She must have hit something important with her gunfire. She heard the faint sound of sirens in the distance. Two law enforcement vehicles raced toward them with lights flashing. The Jeep had stalled on the side of the road. She could barely make out the outline of its driver as he ran in front of the beam of the Jeep's headlights and into the wooded area bordering the interstate.

"Sheriff, stop! We have backup. Let's arrest those guys."

The older man jerked his head toward the back seat, not easing up on the gas. "Why don't you check on your partner, and we'll let my guys take care of the perps. Once they're in custody and processed, we can go to the station and interrogate them."

Randy sat hunched in the corner, his hands gripping his head much like what had happened after she'd first walked into his hospital room.

She eased over the back of the seat and sat

beside him, her hand covering his. "Are you okay? What can I do to help?"

"Nothing. Headache." He inhaled sharply and squeezed his eyes tight.

Panic surged inside her. "We need to get him to a hospital."

"The nearest hospital is the one we just ran from. Do you really want to go back there and take the risk another shooter shows up?" The sheriff glanced over his shoulder. She reluctantly shook her head. "I thought not. The best thing we can do is get him to the cabin so he can rest."

"But—"

"I'll stop at the first convenience store for water and extra-strength headache meds. If he gets worse, I'll contact his doctor and see if she can call in a prescription. Okay?"

Katherine opened her mouth to reply, but Randy spoke up before she could. "Sounds like a good plan. Besides, the doctor said headaches were normal. They should get better with time." He grasped her hand and squeezed it.

Katherine's mind whirled. Why wouldn't the sheriff stop and help arrest the suspects? Or at least take them to another hospital, even one farther away? What was his angle? And what was going on with Randy? One minute he was curled up in pain, and the next he was agreeing with the sheriff.

Katherine wasn't sure if she was ready to trust local law enforcement completely, especially the sheriff. She didn't think he had connections to the illegal horse racing and drug ring, but she suspected he was keeping some secrets of his own. Something wasn't ringing true with the situation. She had a feeling that she was in a race against time in more ways than one.

Mac shifted slightly and attempted to stretch his legs, which proved impossible in the confines of the back seat. What was taking the sheriff so long? He'd been inside the convenience store for almost fifteen minutes. It shouldn't take that long to buy pain reliever.

Had something happened to the lawman? Could the shooters have escaped the other officers and caught up to them again?

Mac craned his neck to get a better view of the store, but to no avail since the sheriff had parked his pickup truck behind a dumpster in the darkest corner of the lot.

A faint snore reached his ear as a soft breath fluttered against his neck. A smile tugged at his mouth. Erin had started yawning shortly after the sheriff parked in the secluded area. A few minutes ago she had announced she was going to "rest her eyes for a minute" and had insisted she wouldn't fall asleep. It was no surprise she had lost the battle to stay awake. He imagined she'd had very little sleep since his disappearance. She must have been so worried about him when she didn't know where he was or what had happened. Add to that the adrenaline rush of running for their lives, and then having to shoot at their pursuers, hanging half inside and half outside a moving vehicle. It amazed him she'd lasted as long as she had.

Mac knew what it felt like coming down off an adrenaline high. He'd experienced it himself many times while in the military and again while going through the academy. The rush was—wait. Where had that thought come from? Which branch of the military had he served in, and what academy had he attended? Law enforcement? Were he and Erin a husband-and-wife law enforcement team? Federal marshals? FBI? CIA? He couldn't remember. The image in his mind's eye was like a blurry photograph that couldn't be brought into full focus. Another fleeting memory that fluttered in just long enough to tease him with some hidden detail from his past. He massaged his temples.

"Head still hurting?" Erin asked softly. Her

eyes remained closed, but the casualness of her demeanor couldn't hide the concern in her tone.

He hated to worry the one person he knew must care about him the most. Mac covered her hand with his. "No. I'm fine. Don't worry so much."

She opened her eyes and leaned over to search his face. "I'm not sure how to do that. Until you regain your full memories, I'm afraid worrying about you is part of the job."

"Is it a job? Being married to me, I mean." He regretted the words as soon as they passed his lips. He didn't want to know the answer, not really. The only memories he had of their time together were of them on their wedding day, of them watching television while eating popcorn and laughing, and of them sharing a prayer before a meal, their hands clasped and heads bowed. He had no memories of arguments or disagreements, but he wasn't naive enough to think they never argued.

She opened her mouth to speak, and he placed a finger on her lips.

"No. Don't answer. It wasn't a fair question. I'm sure there are times marriage feels like a chore, but from this moment forward, I promise to never take you or our marriage for granted. I may not remember much, but I know

I'm very blessed to be alive. And I'm blessed to have you by my side."

She pulled back and gave a half smile. "I can honestly say being your partner hasn't been a hard job."

Partner. He liked that. Partners worked together for a common goal, supported and encouraged each other. A partnership was exactly what a marriage should be. With the loss of his memories, Mac couldn't say that he'd always made wise choices in his life, but it seemed he'd made a smart move when he'd fallen in love with Erin and married her.

Katherine couldn't put it off any longer. She needed to come clean with Randy and tell him the truth. How hard is it to tell someone that you're nothing more than coworkers, maybe a little more than acquaintances but not really friends?

"I know I've been putting off telling you much about…our life. I hoped your memories would return on their own, without having to be forced, but—"

"I know what you're going to say."

"Oh?"

"Yeah. I should have figured it out back at the hospital. How could I have thought we were spies, or that we were in witness protection? Surely if I could remember the aliases we used, I'd also remember our real names, too."

"You would think," she mumbled under her breath, swallowing the nervous laughter that threatened.

"What'd you say?" He leaned close, his whiskered cheek scraping hers.

She'd never seen him with a five-o'clock shadow before. Strangely enough, even though she had hated when her ex-fiancé had gone through a beard phase, she thought the subtle hint of a beard on Randy softened his angular features, especially his slightly square-shaped jaw. Although if she were honest, she would miss the small dimple in his chin if he grew a full beard.

She swallowed. "Um. Nothing. You were saying?"

"I know we're in law enforcement."

"You do?"

"Yes. My only question is which branch?"

"We're federal agents." If he'd figured out the law enforcement part, she didn't see a need to withhold that detail from him.

"FBI." He looked thoughtful for a moment and then nodded, as if in affirmation. "That sounds right. So, we're working undercover?"

"Oh, I'm so glad you've figured it out. I wasn't sure how to tell you—"

"Just one more question. How were we able to convince our superiors to let us work on this assignment together? I mean, is it common practice to let husband-and-wife agents work together on a mission? I would think there would be concern that one or the other might let their guard down and put themselves and their spouse in danger." He gasped. "Wait a minute. Is that what happened? I let my guard down because I was worried about protecting you?"

The driver's side door opened, and a blast of cold air invaded the otherwise warm space. The sheriff leaned in, holding a bag in one hand and a drink carrier in the other. "I thought you guys might be hungry. Not knowing what you'd want to eat, I gathered an assortment of day-old pastries, hot dogs, chips and strong coffee."

"Sounds good to me," Katherine said, thankful for the interruption. "The last thing I ate was a pastry I grabbed as I headed to the hospital this morning."

"That's not good. You mustn't sacrifice your health because of your concern for me." Randy reached across the front seat and took the drink carrier, offering a foam cup full of strong, tar-colored coffee to her.

"I wasn't hungry." She shrugged. "I meant to get some dinner from the hospital cafeteria, but I didn't want to leave you while you were sleeping. Then those guys showed up…" Katherine let her voice trail off. Why had she said that? *I didn't want to leave you while you were sleeping.* She sounded like the lovestruck, concerned wife Randy thought her to be. One who wouldn't eat or leave his side until she knew he was okay. Feeling the need to clarify, she added, "I'm not really a morning person. Besides, I'm usually not hungry until noon."

"Here. We can't have you fainting from hunger." The sheriff tossed the bag of food into her lap, plucked a cup of coffee out of the carrier, slid into the driver's seat and started the vehicle. A smile on his otherwise stern face.

Was the older lawman making fun of her? No. She didn't think he was. If Katherine were any judge of character, which in her youth may have been in doubt but in recent years—at least where her career was concerned—had seemed to improve, she would imagine Sheriff Walker was sympathizing with her plight. After all, even local law enforcement had days where they were working a difficult case and couldn't readily take care of their own needs, like food or a nap.

Randy unwrapped a hot dog, opened a mustard packet and applied a thin line of the yellow condiment to the length of the hot dog. Then he opened a ketchup packet and repeated the process, adding twice the amount of the sweet red condiment, then handed the hot dog to her with a napkin.

She was dumbfounded. Even though they had probably only eaten hot dogs three or four times since they'd started working together, Randy remembered how she liked hers.

Taking a big bite, she chewed slowly, her mind deep in thought. She had noticed while working with Randy that he seemed to have a photographic memory—no, that probably wasn't the correct terminology. It wasn't like he could skim a page and remember every word on it, but he seemed to have a knack for zeroing in on details in every social or work situation. Even when he didn't realize he was doing it, he was a whiz at picking up on clues. The only reason they had been able to trace Torres and his illegal horse racing ring to Dove Creek, Wyoming, was because Randy had remembered seeing a matchbook Torres had dropped at the last race in Blackberry Falls, Colorado, the day before he disappeared.

She could only hope Randy's keen observation skills had picked up on something at the time of his accident. And that the memories of what he'd witnessed weren't lost forever.

FIVE

Mac dried his face and peered into the oval mirror that hung over the pedestal sink in the small, but functioning, bathroom. It was amazing what a shower, a change of clothes—even borrowed ones that were a bit baggy—and a fresh shave could do to make a person feel better.

He sniffed. The smell of coffee and bacon filled the air. Guess that meant someone else was awake.

They'd arrived at the two-bedroom cabin in the wee hours of the morning. And, even though he and Erin were husband and wife, the sheriff had insisted on sleeping on the couch so Mac could have one room and Erin the other.

He had tried to protest, but the sheriff had pierced him with a stern glare. "One of your headaches might keep her up. Doesn't she deserve undisturbed rest? Hasn't she been through enough looking for you the last few days and then being shot at?"

All of Mac's fight had gone out of him. He'd kissed Erin's forehead, and she'd gone into the separate room and closed the door.

Hopefully, she was awake. He had so many questions, and they had no time to lose if they wanted to catch the guys chasing them. Tossing the damp towel over the shower curtain bar, he opened the door and stepped into the hall at the same time Erin came out of the bedroom, her wavy brown hair pulled back off her face in a ponytail, accentuating high cheekbones and striking blue-green eyes. He couldn't imagine ever growing tired of looking at her. She appeared well rested, but there were faint dark circles under her eyes, making him feel like a heel for not fully understanding how right the sheriff was to insist she have undisturbed rest.

"Good morning. How are you feeling?" she asked softly, making the shoe-box-sized hallway seem like an intimate corner in a crowded restaurant.

His mouth went dry, and his heart hammered against his rib cage. His wife had to be the most beautiful woman in the world. *Thank You, Lord, for my blessings. Please help me remember every moment of the life I've shared with this woman.* The prayer had come without preamble or thought, giving him a sense of comfort. Mac might not have many memories of his life, but he liked what he knew so far. He was a Christian, a husband and an FBI agent.

"Do you still have a headache?" Erin continued before he answered her previous question.

He should have spoken first, instead of standing there in a daze. If he wasn't careful, she would really think his brain was addled.

"I'm fine. Did you sleep well?"

"Eh, so-so. It was hard to shut off my brain, but I managed a couple of hours sleep." She smiled. "I see you found a razor."

"I did." He rubbed his jaw. "Wait a minute. Do I normally wear a beard?"

Laughter rang out as her smile broadened. "No. You're not a beard kind of guy. You look…" She leaned in closer, searching his face. "Actually, you look rested, which is a good thing. I'm guessing you slept well."

"Alright, you two. If you're done jawin', can we sit down and eat before the bacon and eggs get cold?" Sheriff Walker glared at them from the open-concept main living area.

Mac stepped aside to let Erin pass, and they joined the older lawman at the kitchen island.

Sheriff Walker motioned for them to sit on the two barstools that were positioned on one side of the island and placed plates heaped with bacon, scrambled eggs and toast in front of them. "Here you go. Eat up. You'll need your strength to catch those guys chasing you."

"What do you mean, catch them? Did your deputies let them slip through their hands last night?" Anger sparkled in Erin's eyes.

Mac imagined his wife was a force to be reckoned with when she was fired up.

The sheriff bristled. "Hold on there, missy. Don't you disrespect my deputies. It's not like you've been successful at catching these guys and putting them behind bars. It's a wonder they didn't open fire in the hospital last night, killing innocent people. You can just come off your high-and-mighty federal agent high horse. I have top-notch law enforcement officers on my team. They'll find the trail and catch them. I can promise you that."

"No, Sheriff, you hold on. And don't be talking to my wife in that tone." Mac pushed his stool back and stood, towering over the other man. "She wasn't trying to disrespect your men. She's fired up, but she has a right to be when someone is trying to kill us."

"FWEET!" A whistle rent the air and both men turned to face Erin, who had stood at the same time Mac had.

She placed a hand on Mac's arm. "Thank

you for defending me, but it's okay." Turning to the sheriff, she added, "You're right. I have no business questioning your officers' abilities. It's just that I had hoped we were a step closer to closing this case. I'm sorry."

She picked up the coffee carafe, poured two cups and topped them off with cream and sugar. Handing one to him, she sat back down and took a bite of eggs. "Mmm. These are really good, Sheriff."

Mac stood his ground, refusing to be the first to back down. He didn't know if he had always had a stubborn streak or if it was simply because of his memory loss. The past twenty-four hours had left him feeling helpless and insecure in his abilities, but he never wanted to appear weak in front of Erin.

The sheriff grunted and turned back to the stove to fill his own plate.

Erin tugged at Mac's sleeve and whispered, "You won the standoff. You can eat now."

As if to punctuate her words, his stomach picked that moment to emit a loud rumble. He looked down just in time to see the smile on her lips before she ducked her head and put another forkful of eggs into her mouth.

Settling back onto the stool, he picked up his fork. He would eat. But once breakfast was over, he would get answers. After all, Mac had just figured out he had a stubborn streak. This was the day he would stand his ground and get answers. No more allowing Erin to put him off.

This is the day which the Lord hath made; we will rejoice and be glad in it. Mac's fork froze halfway to his mouth. Where had that thought come from? He knew it was a Bible verse. Perhaps he'd learned it in Sunday school as a young child. Why couldn't he remember his parents? He didn't even know if he had siblings. It was time to fill in the dark holes in his memory. He needed answers, and he needed them today.

Katherine took another sip of coffee as she observed the men in the room. She wasn't used to having someone defend her the way Randy had earlier. Other men she'd spent time with had always figured as a federal agent she could handle her own battles, which in most cases was true. But even independent, career-oriented women liked to feel cherished sometimes. The calm, matter-of-fact way Randy had spoken had been bone-chilling, way more intimidating than Sheriff Walker's angry rant. It had been nice to have a man care enough to jump to her defense.

No, not just any man. Randy.

The partner she'd worked with for almost

a year, a dedicated agent who fought for what he believed in and would go to the ends of the earth for those he loved. Hadn't she seen that dedication in the way he'd worked tirelessly to track down Torres's illegal horse racing ring again? And it wasn't just because he wanted to take down the cartel behind the races that were a front for drugs, money laundering and, most likely, human trafficking. It was also because he wanted justice for Trevor's death. The partner who had been like an older brother to him. The one who had given him the wristwatch he wore, the item he refused to take off even though it was most likely damaged beyond repair in the accident. Randy Ingalls fought for those he cared about. If she were being honest with herself, she had to admit when he had so readily jumped to her defense her heart had done a funny little flip-flop-flutter, even if he had only defended her so vehemently because he thought they were married.

If she hadn't been so standoffish with her coworkers through the years, could she have built close relationships with them? Maybe she could have formed a few ties that would have felt like family, like Randy and Trevor.

After her almost-marriage ten years ago, she'd dedicated her life to her career and was content being alone. Her mom, a stay-at-home wife and mother who found herself divorced in her early forties and having to figure out how to support two daughters on her own, had taught Katherine and her sister to be self-sufficient and not build their entire world around a man—a lesson Katherine hadn't fully understood until the day she'd been stood up at the altar. That's why the sheer fact that Randy's defending her had caused her heart to flutter scared her more than the men with guns who were chasing them.

Get a grip and focus. Katherine blinked and pulled herself back to the present. She didn't need a man defending her. Besides, the entire thing had been her fault. She knew better than to imply local law enforcement officers weren't competent, even if it was unintentional and not at all the way she truly felt.

While she still thought the sheriff was withholding details, she no longer doubted his desire to help them. One thing bugged her, though. Why had Wanda given away their cover?

"You ready to tell me what brought you to my county?" Sheriff Walker's question pulled her from her thoughts.

"I can't disclose any information regarding our investigation unless I'm given a direct order from my superior."

Sheriff Walker laughed. "Wanda told me you'd say that. She also said you two are two of the best agents the Bureau has."

Katherine placed her empty mug on the counter and watched as the older officer picked it up and loaded it into the small dishwasher. "Are you ready to tell me how you found out our—" She'd almost said *undercover identities* but didn't want to field a ton of questions from Randy in front of the sheriff. "Um. How you found out our identities?"

"Don't worry. *You* didn't give away your identity at the hospital. Most people wouldn't have even caught on, but you see…" Sheriff Walker turned toward her and Randy and shrugged. "I'm a retired US marshal. Making up backgrounds to fit a narrative is—was—my specialty."

Okay, she hadn't seen that one coming. "That still doesn't explain how you could get the information out of SAC Richardson."

"Wanda and I worked together on a case, a long time ago. We developed a close bond. You might say Wanda was the one who got away." A smile lifted the corner of his mouth, and he got a faraway look in his eyes. "Anyway, after meeting you at the hospital, I made some phone calls to contacts at the Marshals' office and the FBI. I didn't know if I was dealing with a witness protection situation or if it was an undercover operation. All I knew was, no matter the truth, you were in my town. And with your partner injured and possibly having amnesia, things could get serious, fast."

"So, you called SAC Richardson, and she just told you everything?" Katherine watched Randy in her peripheral vision as he jotted down notes. She wasn't exactly sure where he had found paper and pen, but it did not surprise her he had them. He was an analytical person and preferred to handwrite everything when processing the details of a case. Maybe taking notes now would help jog his memory.

"Come on, Agent Lewis, you know better than that." The sheriff's eyes widened at her intake of breath.

"Who's Agent Lewis?" Randy asked, his pen in midair. Turning to her with a look of shock on his face, he asked, "Why would he call you that? You kept your maiden name after we married?" He shook his head. "No. Lewis isn't your maiden name. It's Chambers."

Randy got up and paced, then turned back to glare at them. "Would someone, *please*, tell me the truth? I don't care that the doctor said my memories need to come back on their own. I'm tired of the lies, and I don't believe being told the truth will destroy me." He sat back down beside Katherine and picked up her hand. "Didn't you take vows…in sickness and in health? Well, this is the 'in sickness' part. Help me remember, because without my memories, I can't protect you from the people trying to kill us."

Katherine's heart jumped into her throat, making it difficult to swallow. His anguish was evident. She had no clue who the woman with the last name of Chambers was. Most likely someone from his past. Was he married before? Had he confused memories from his past with memories from the present?

Sheriff Walker cleared his throat. "I'll take that as my cue to leave. I need to go to the office and see what leads I can track down. Wanda didn't go into specifics, but she said your case is connected to the illegal horse racing that's been plaguing our state the last couple of years. I'm going to grab a few files from my desk with names of people I think may be linked to your case. Local law enforcement all up and down the state have been working to shut down the illegal match races, and the activities surrounding them. I don't have enough evidence to convict anyone. However, if we work together and share files, we may make the connection that solves this case." Turning back to Katherine, he asked, "Do you need anything from town?"

"Yes, please." She raised a foot and wiggled her toes. "Shoes would be nice. And I need a burner phone. I lost my cell phone somewhere last night, and I need to call Wanda."

"Oh, wait." Randy jumped up and jogged into the bedroom he'd slept in the night before, returning with her phone in his hand. "I found this on my hospital room floor after you ran out last night. I'm sorry, I forgot to give it back."

"It's okay. Thanks." She looked the phone over and made sure it still functioned properly. "Looks like it's working. But I need a charger."

"Will one of these work?" the sheriff asked. He opened a drawer and pulled out a variety of chargers. "It seems like every time I invite friends out here to fish, they end up leaving behind phone cords. I keep telling them to leave their devices at home. This is a place to disconnect and unwind."

She laughed and selected the appropriate cord. "Thank you."

Sheriff Walker clapped Randy on the back of his shoulder. "I can only imagine how frustrating it would be to wake up with no memories, but try to cut her some slack. She's doing the best she can."

Turning to Katherine, the older lawman smiled. "It's obvious you two work well together. Even without his memories, he's had your back and been a true partner. Trust your gut, but don't forget to trust him, too. In dangerous situations, I can almost guarantee you his training will kick in and his reactions will be instinctive."

She hoped Sheriff Walker was right. Katherine needed Randy's memories to return. If they didn't, she at least needed him to recall his training. She couldn't do this alone.

"Okay, guys, it's almost noon. I need to get going. I'll try not to be gone over three or four hours." Sheriff Walker headed to the door. "Oh, if you want to go fishing, there are extra rods and gear in the attic. The access door is in the hall. Just pull the string to lower the steps. You know, fishing is a great way to clear your mind and make things come into focus." He turned and left, whistling a tune as he went.

Katherine wasn't sure about fishing, but she knew one thing. If the look Randy was giving her was any indication, the next few hours were going to be a difficult, treacherous journey through the cobwebs of his mind. How was he going to take it when he discovered the memories he thought were real were nothing more than play acting?

* * *

Mac looked over the notes he'd jotted down earlier.

WHAT I'VE LEARNED
I'm An FBI Agent
Undercover
Erin's Last Name = Lewis
Sheriff Walker Is An Ex–US Marshal
Someone Wants Me & Erin Dead!!

QUESTIONS I HAVE
Sac (Meaning?)
Who Is Wanda Richardson?
Whose Last Name Is Chambers?
How Did Erin And I Meet?
Where Is The Rest Of My Family?

Mac fingered the wristwatch he wore, tracing the jagged, cracked line that spread out from the center of the crystal, and added another question. WHY IS THE WATCH IMPORTANT?

Where had he gotten the wristwatch? It looked to be very old. Its army green nylon band was frayed and worn with age, and the silver casing on the watch itself had tarnished from years of wear. Unfastening the band, he turned the watch over in his hands. There was something engraved on the back. He twisted it every which way, bringing the watch close to his face and then holding it at arm's length. The words were barely visible, the etching worn away through the years.

He moved to the kitchen window and held the watch in the sunlight, but he still couldn't make out the words. Looking around, his eyes fell on the notepad he'd been using. When he was a young boy playing detective, he had often gotten in trouble for using a paper and pencil trick to read notes his mother had written. Would the same trick work on a watch?

He took a step, then paused and shook his head. No time to rejoice at a newly recalled memory, or to wonder where it had come from. He opened the drawer on the side of the island where he'd located the pad and pen earlier. Rummaging around, he located a pencil with broken lead. Unable to find a pencil sharpener, he took a knife out of the block on the counter and whittled a point. Not perfect, but it would do.

Placing the watch facedown on the countertop, he turned to the middle of the notepad and ripped out a blank sheet of paper. Then he placed it over the watch and rubbed the edge of the pencil lead over it. Words and numbers appeared on the paper. TYPE A-11, followed by a serial number, an order number and the name of the watchmaker. Then, in tiny print, he discovered a long-forgotten message—

To: James
Love, Martha

Who were James and Martha, and what was their connection to him? A heavy sigh escaped from deep within him, but instead of easing the weight of the lost memories pressing down on him, it seemed to act as a reminder that the burden of not knowing his past would only become heavier with each passing day. Each piece of the puzzle he uncovered only seemed to bring more questions that needed to be answered.

Thankfully, he wasn't alone. He had his wife, and according to what Sheriff Walker had said, she was one of the best FBI agents in the business. With her on his side, what did he have to fear?

For God hath not given us the spirit of fear; but of power, and of love, and of a sound mind. 2 Timothy 1:7. The Bible verse echoed in his brain, bringing a smile to Mac's lips. Some memories brought strength. God would lead the way.

He started absentmindedly doodling on the

bottom of the paper with his notes. When he finished, he picked up the page and studied the image. Two horses racing around an oval track. What did the image mean? He quickly started jotting down all the words that came to mind—DIRT TRACK, HORSE RACING, GAMBLING, DRUGS, MONEY LAUNDERING, HUMAN TRAFFICKING.

"What are you working on?" Erin's question startled him, and he jumped, bumping her jaw with his shoulder.

"Oh, I'm sorry!" He winced at the sight of the big red spot that had already formed on her face. With her fair complexion, it was sure to bruise. "Let me get some ice."

"No. I'm fine. Really." She smiled, easing his anxiety. "I shouldn't have snuck up on you like that."

"It's alright. Are you sure you're okay?" He touched her jaw, and she jerked back. Surely, he hadn't hurt her so badly that she'd be sensitive to a simple touch. Mac searched her eyes. Was his wife afraid of him?

Her smile broadened, but didn't quite reach her eyes. "Really. I'm okay. And I'm ready to go fishing." She did a slow turn in front of him, showing off the jeans, rolled at the ankle, and the blue plaid flannel shirt she was wearing.

"Nice outfit. Where'd you find it?"

"In the closet. I'm guessing they belong to the sheriff's wife or daughter maybe." She shrugged. "He told us to make ourselves at home, so I don't imagine he'll mind me borrowing clothes." She looked at her feet. "Only I didn't find any shoes. I guess I'll have to go barefoot a while longer."

"Hang on. I may have something that'll work, at least outdoors." He made his way to the hall and opened the hatch to the attic. He'd seen several pairs of rubber boots up there when he brought down the fishing poles and lures while she hunted for something to wear. Mac quickly climbed the ladder, searched for the smallest pair of boots for her and grabbed a pair for himself, then descended back down the ladder while trying to balance the things he carried in his hands.

"Ta-da." He held up his treasures.

A memory flashed in his mind like an old movie playing in slow motion. He was in his early twenties with a big grin plastered on his face as he proudly displayed a large catfish. A tent and campfire were to his right, and a river was behind him. His wife backed away from him, with her palms facing forward and shaking her head. "I'm not cooking that. I told you I don't like smelly fish." He took a step toward her, and she squealed and ducked into the tent. "I'm done. I want to go home. This is the worst honeymoon ever!"

"Mac. Are you okay?" Erin's voice pulled him back to the present.

He blinked to clear his vision and tilted his head to see her beautiful, concerned face. "Why didn't you tell me we aren't married? That I'm married to someone else? Where is my wife?"

SIX

Katherine's jaw dropped. Randy really was married. A thousand questions raced through her mind as she tried to process what she'd just heard. Why hadn't he ever mentioned his wife before? Did he have children, too? What did she really know about him outside of work? The answer was nothing.

They had never discussed anything that wasn't related to the case. Just like it had been with every other partner she'd worked with since leaving the academy. And she liked it that way, or so she'd told herself. Do your job. Solve the case. Move on. No attachments.

Her life was easier when she kept her co-workers at bay and didn't form close friendships. Hadn't she learned the hard way not to mix work life with her personal life when Nelson left her at the altar? Not only because they were attending the academy together when they'd started dating, but also because well-meaning coworkers and friends could ask extremely difficult and personal questions. Like, hadn't she seen any signs the relationship had been on rocky ground? Or why, after all these years, was she still single? Didn't she want to have kids and a family of her own?

It suddenly hit her that setting such strict boundaries with her coworkers also meant she knew nothing about them. And, right now, that was a tremendous disadvantage.

"I'm sorry. I don't know the answer to your question." She took a step toward Randy. He backed away, a look of distrust on his face. "We've been partners for almost a year, but you've never discussed your personal life with me. I've never met your family."

He dropped the rubber boots onto the stone hearth of the fireplace, sank down onto the oversize faux cowhide chair positioned at an angle in front of it and rubbed his temples.

Another headache brought on by the shock? "I really am sorry. I didn't know what to do when I found you at the hospital and the only memories you had were of our undercover identities."

"You mean my name isn't really Mac? It's all been a lie?"

She nodded, helplessly. There was no excuse. She should have told him the truth sooner.

The chime of her cell phone alerted her to a text message. SAC Richardson requested she call her ASAP.

"Special Agent in Charge Wanda Richardson wants me to call her. I'll answer your questions when I return."

Not giving him a chance to reply, she went out the back door of the cabin and sat on a deck chair, putting as much distance between herself and Randy as she dared. In his current state, she hated leaving his side even for a moment, but she also hoped Wanda could give her guidance on how to proceed. If anyone knew details of Randy's private life, it would be their superior.

Answering on the first ring, Wanda demanded, "Katherine, are you okay? How's Randy?"

"We're fine. Both of us." It was basically the truth. Physically, they were fine. Emotionally drained, though she could only speak for herself in that area. Katherine was in a state of disbelief, and she could only imagine that Randy's emotions were more mixed up than hers.

"Grant Walker said Randy has amnesia."

"He does, but it seems some of his memories are returning." Katherine pressed the phone closer to her ear. "Can you get in contact with his wife? He's eager to know that she's okay."

"Randy isn't married."

"He isn't?"

"Not that I'm aware of. I recall hearing something years ago about him being divorced, but I don't know any details."

"Well, that's not good. He has lots of questions, and I have a feeling he isn't going to be happy if I can't provide answers."

"Give him the answers that you know. Don't sugarcoat it or hide anything. Randy is a very intelligent man. He'll be able to process it all in his own way. Hopefully, his full memory will return sooner rather than later. Hang on, someone's at my door." Katherine heard muffled voices as her superior spoke to whoever had entered her office. A few seconds later, she returned. "Okay, sorry. Now, where were we? Oh, yeah. Do you think Randy is capable of completing the assignment?"

"Yes. I do," she replied without hesitation. Randy Ingalls was one of the most competent agents she knew, and in the past twenty-four hours she'd witnessed his instinctive ability to do his job even when he didn't realize he was doing it.

"Okay. Well, I'm going to trust you on that. But before I let you go, there's one other thing." Wanda paused, as if deciding how to phrase her next thought. "I had Sheriff Walker send me the report on Randy's accident. It's eerily similar to the accident that claimed the life of Agent Trevor Douglas. So much so, that I am convinced we have a mole in the agency."

Katherine gasped involuntarily.

"I know. I didn't want to admit it, but the cartel has stayed a step ahead of us at every stage in this investigation. They always know when we're getting close to taking them down. We've lost one agent. I don't want to lose another. Watch your back. In the meantime, keep all communication to a minimum. Got it?"

"Yes, ma'am. But before you go, can you tell me why you trusted Sheriff Walker with our identities?"

"Are you questioning the way I do my job?"

"No, ma'am. Not at all. I simply need to know if we can trust Sheriff Walker."

A sigh sounded across the line. "I have no reason to believe he's anything but trustworthy."

"He said you worked a case together a long time ago." Now, why had she felt the need to bring that up? Was she trying to irritate her superior?

"Yes. A long time ago. Almost twenty years to be exact." Wanda cleared her throat. "I believe Grant Walker is a good guy. But as always, trust your gut. Don't share more than necessary until it becomes evident that it's needed."

Katherine disconnected the call, her mind even more unsettled after the conversation than it had been before. One thing at a time. Step one, find the mole. She mentally ran through a list of her coworkers, trying to pinpoint who could be a mole. Not a single name stood out to her. The members of the team were dedicated agents who worked hard to take the bad guys off the streets.

A cold breeze rustled the trees, causing a dip in the temperature and sending a shiver down her spine. She stood and scanned the woods. No obvious sign of danger lurking in the shadows helped tamp down the uneasy feeling that threatened to take hold. Inhaling a deep breath and slowly blowing it out, she quietly walked back into the cabin, locking the door behind her. She twisted the knob to make sure it was secure.

Randy was still seated in the oversize chair. "Who am I?" he asked, barely above a whisper, without moving.

The question came at her like a snake strike with a direct hit to her heart. Her lungs burned as she forced big gulps of air into them, willing herself to speak. He looked up at her, questions in his eyes that she knew she'd never be able to answer. All she could do was give him the facts, as she knew them to be.

"Your name is Randy Ingalls. You're forty-two years old. You're an ex-army Green Beret." Knowing he'd want to take notes, she handed him the notepad and pen he'd left on the kitchen island. "You've been a federal agent for fourteen years, but we've only worked together for eleven months."

"Have you met any of my family?"

"No." She puffed out a breath. *Lord, please help me choose the correct words.* "I asked SAC Richardson about your wife. She said you were divorced before you joined the Bureau. She doesn't know your former wife's name or how to contact her. I'm sorry."

He worked his jaw, and the vein in his neck twitched. "I appreciate the effort."

She wasn't sure which was worse, the frustration in his expression when she'd reentered the cabin or his attempt to sound indifferent now. It was time for her vow not to nose into her coworkers' personal lives to be broken. If Randy's memories hadn't fully returned by the time they wrapped the case up, she would dig into his past and find a family member—past or present—who could answer his questions.

Turning back to his notes, he continued, "I know your last name is Lewis, because Sheriff Walker let it slip this morning, but what's your first name?"

"Katherine." She smiled, and her lips quivered. *Come on, Katherine, where's that thick skin Dad kept telling you to develop? Stop feeling sorry for the situation and do your job.* "Special Agent Katherine Lewis, at your service. I've been an agent for ten years, but like I said, we've been partners for less than a year. Your former partner, Trevor Douglas, was killed in a suspicious car accident two weeks before the Bureau transferred me to the case."

The pen flew across the paper as he took notes, word for word. "Suspicious accident? Was his death connected to the case?"

"It's believed so. There were no witnesses. Based on the tire tracks at the scene, they forced his vehicle over the side of the mountain. Also," she swallowed. This next bit of information was always the hardest to digest. "It's suspected someone planted a bomb in the trunk of his vehicle that would explode on impact. Along with an accelerant, providing the necessary fuel to create a heat so intense the fire destroyed all evidence, including the body."

"What can you tell me about the case we're working on?" His lack of response concerning the murder of his former partner was a bit unsettling, even though she knew it was only because he didn't remember Trevor. Wanda had told Katherine about Randy and Trevor's bond of brotherhood when she received the assignment, letting her know she had big shoes to fill.

"There's an illegal horse racing ring that's been making the rounds in Colorado and Wyoming for the past few years. It came to the Bureau's attention a little over two years ago, after we rescued sixteen young people from a human trafficking ring in Denver. There's a strong likelihood the two groups are connected and that they're both run by the León Dormido Cartel that has connections to Mexico and the United States. You've been on the case from the beginning."

Randy got up and crossed to the island, returning with another sheet of paper. "I guess that explains this drawing I made while you were getting ready. At first, I thought it was mindless doodling. Then all these thoughts came out of nowhere, so I started jotting them down." He showed her the list he'd made to the side.

"What's this?" She pointed to what appeared to be smudged pencil markings on the top of the page.

"It's a tracing of the words engraved on the back of my watch."

She examined the markings. "Do you know who James and Martha are?"

"No." He sighed and shoved his hand through his hair. "I really need to get to a computer so I can do some research."

"You're right. I had thought we might stay here for a couple of days, to give you time to recover. But that's probably not the best move. When the sheriff returns, we'll have him drive us to the hospital to pick up the rental car. Then we can go to the safe house where I've hidden our laptop and files and formulate a plan."

Randy instinctively looked at his watch. "Ugh. I keep forgetting it's broken."

"Why don't you take it off until you can get it to a repair shop?"

"Because for some reason, the watch gives me a strange sense of purpose. You know? Like it's a reminder to work hard to get justice for people who have been wronged."

"I get that." She pulled her phone out of her back pocket and checked the time. "The sheriff has only been gone an hour and a half. That means we have at least two hours until he returns."

Randy smiled. "So, let's go fishing. Maybe the sheriff is right and it will help clear my mind of unnecessary clutter, leaving room for my memories to return."

They slipped into the rubber boots. Then Randy gathered the fishing rods and tackle box he'd rounded up while she'd been getting ready, and they stepped outside.

The cabin sat in the middle of a clearing, with a thickly wooded area on both sides and a stream fifty yards or so from the back deck. Ominous, dark storm clouds were beginning to gather in the distance. Would they even have time to get their fishing hooks wet before the storms rolled in?

With the soil already saturated from the winter thaw and the heavy rains that had moved across the area the night of Randy's accident, a thunderstorm could prevent them leaving the area. Katherine hoped the sheriff would return quickly so they could make it back to the safe house before the storm began.

They were crossing the backyard at a diagonal, headed toward the rocky path that led to the stream, and had just cleared the side of the cabin, giving them a clear view of the front yard, when Randy heard a vehicle coming up the half-mile-long drive that wound through the woods. "That can't be the sheriff returning. He hasn't had time to make it to the station and back."

"I was thinking the same thing. We need to get out of sight."

Randy quickly assessed the situation. The stream was closest, but the trees and foliage around the section directly behind the cabin were too sparse to offer much protection. And with the sound of the engine becoming louder with each passing second, running across the clearing toward the wooded area was not an option. "Back inside," he ordered.

"Are there two vehicles?" Katherine asked.

"Sounds like an ATV coming through the woods on the other side. Hurry!" They raced across the yard, bounded up the steps, crossed the deck and pushed into the cabin, locking the dead bolt behind them. "Hang on. Don't move." He grasped Katherine's arm before she could step off the mat positioned just inside the door.

"What? Why?" she questioned breathlessly.

He took a few deep breaths, his lungs burning from the exertion. "If we track up the floor with the wet grass clinging to our boots, we'll lead them straight to us."

"Where exactly are we supposed to hide in a cabin that's roughly eight hundred square feet?" The fire he had seen earlier was back in her eyes. "Should we call 911?"

"When we drove in last night, it seemed we were pretty far from everything. I doubt they'd make it here in time to offer assistance."

"Okay. I'll get my gun from the bedroom and try to hold them off."

"Remove your boots. Leave them on the mat. I'll meet you in the hall. Oh, and grab our clothes and anything else that might show we've been here."

She did as he ordered, leaving her boots on the mat and racing across the cabin on her bare feet.

Randy stuck the fishing poles in a wicker umbrella basket beside the door and slid the tackle box under the bench beside it. Then he slipped out of his boots, scooped the mat up and carried the bundle to the alcove off the kitchen that housed the washer and dryer. Lifting the lid to the washer, he dumped everything inside and prayed anyone looking for them wouldn't waste time checking the laundry.

Maybe the vehicles belonged to neighbors or friends of the sheriff and weren't the men who chased them last night. Crossing to the front window, he peeked through the blinds. There went that thought. A black SUV pulled to a stop in front of the cabin, and the man with red hair from the hospital last night rounded the house on an ATV, pulling up to the driver's side of the SUV to talk to the men inside.

Spurred into action, Randy crossed to the kitchen, grabbed a paring knife out of the utensil drawer, then snatched his tennis shoes off the floor where he'd left them when he changed into the rubber boots earlier and headed into the hall. Erin was coming out of the room he'd slept in the night before, the clothes he'd commandeered at the hospital in her arms along with her outfit from the day before.

"Now what?"

"We're going up." He pulled on the string to the attic access door and lowered the steps. He motioned for her to lead the way. "After you."

She hesitated for a split second, as if weighing their options, but then she nodded and started climbing.

The sound of the ATV circling the cabin echoed off the walls, the windows shaking more and more with each trip the person made around the building. Was the driver getting closer and closer to the cabin in an attempt to force them out?

One thing was for sure, their attackers weren't trying to sneak up on them. They knew

Randy and Katherine wouldn't have any place to hide, so they were toying with them.

Unfastening the leather belt Sheriff Walker had loaned him, he quickly slipped it off and looped it around the rung of the ladder just above the first folding joint, stretching it over as many of the rungs as he could. Then he used the knife to cut off the string that was used to pull the hatch open and shoved it into his front pocket.

Randy scaled the ladder. Once inside the attic, he lay on his stomach and leaned his upper body through the opening, praying he could reach the end of the belt.

"I've got you," Katherine whispered as she grasped his ankles, keeping him from falling in much the same way as he had her the night before. Her actions encouraged him. He could do this.

Stretching, he wrapped his hand around the leather strap and pulled with all his might. The ladder came up, but the sections didn't bend the way they needed in order for the hatch to close. No. This has to work. His heartbeat pounded in his ears, competing with the sound of the men trying to break down the front door.

He puffed out a breath. One. Two. Three. Randy pulled the belt, and when the ladder was almost parallel with the ceiling, he yanked the strap again. This time the ladder folded correctly. Grasping the sides of the wooden frame, he pulled it closed, but not before he heard the front door of the cabin bust open.

Holding a finger to his lips, he met Katherine's eyes. She nodded understanding and positioned herself in a seated position facing the trapdoor. With her gun in her hand, she sat as motionless as a statue.

Randy continued to lie on his stomach, his ear pressed to the floor. Footsteps grew louder as the men entered the hall, and bedroom doors slammed against walls as they were pushed open.

"Where are they?" a deep, masculine voice demanded. "You said you tracked them here."

"Yes, boss. They have to be here. Somewhere," a nervous-sounding voice insisted. "The sheriff left earlier, but the Feds weren't with him."

More heavy footsteps and slammed doors as they searched every corner of the cabin. "Well, if they're not here, they have to be in the woods. Go tell Greg to stop joyriding the ATV and search for them. You go with him. I'll take the SUV back to my vehicle and meet you guys at the ranch once you've caught them."

"Yes, sir."

"I mean it. Don't stop searching until you

find Ingalls and his partner. I don't care if it takes you all day and all night. Got it? I will not—" The front door slammed, cutting off the remaining words.

Randy and Katherine crawled over to the small window that overlooked the front yard.

"Do you recognize them?" he asked in a hushed tone, though he doubted the men could hear him from outside with the ATV motor still running.

"I don't know who the tall, dark-haired man is, the one they called boss. I've never seen him before, but—"

"Really? His was the one voice that felt familiar to me. Every time he spoke, I kept thinking I should know his name, especially after he said mine." He studied the man in question. Approximately six feet tall, with dark-colored eyes, brown hair and a mustache and goatee. "How did he know my name?"

"I don't know. It's troubling that he knows who you are and not just your alias. He's never shown up on any of the data that I've seen. I know the other two, though." Katherine pointed and Randy leaned forward to peer out at the big, burly man in his mid to late forties with thinning hair. "That's Antonio Torres. He's the one who runs the illegal match races, but he's just a front man and not the person in charge. The guy on the ATV is named Greg. I don't recall his last name right offhand. He's a hired hand, following orders but no power to give them. He hooked up with Torres last spring when they were running races in Blackberry Falls."

"Why weren't we able to capture them last year if we got close enough to know all that information?" He knew his memory was still fuzzy, but surely if they had the names of most of the people involved in the illegal activities, they could have captured them by now.

At his question, Katherine scooted back and sat against the wall, a pensive look on her face. "It was my fault. I left my post as a lookout. The local police chief, Evan Bradshaw, was also at the race doing undercover work, along with the local veterinarian, Grace Porter, whose sister was in the hospital fighting for her life after she was brutally attacked. Dr. Porter interrupted the killer, and he turned his attention onto her." Katherine got a faraway look on her face, as if she were reliving the events of that day. "I was in the SUV with orders to follow Torres if he left the event. I saw Chief Bradshaw and Dr. Porter running through the parking lot to their vehicle, with Greg chasing after them and Torres yelling from the entrance. Without even thinking, I drove my vehicle in their direction and blocked Greg, allowing the chief and Dr. Porter to get away.

"Unfortunately, the distraction I caused provided Torres the opportunity to slip away unnoticed. You were so angry, telling me that my actions had allowed evil men to continue doing bad deeds and, while my actions *may or may not* have saved a life, numerous people would die as a result of the drugs being pushed by Torres and his goons." She looked up at him, and the sadness in her eyes was almost his undoing.

"You were right. Even though I knew you'd been in communication with the chief, I had no business getting sidetracked by a local law enforcement case when my attention should have been on my assignment. I'll never be able to forgive myself for allowing these men to go free for almost a year, forcing countless people into the human trafficking trade and providing others the drugs used to overdose." Her words hit like a sucker punch to the gut.

How could he have been so brutal and thoughtless to a fellow agent who had acted to save a life that was in immediate danger? Maybe he didn't want to regain all of his memories after all, especially if it meant he would recall moments where his Christianity hadn't shone through.

SEVEN

Katherine snapped a couple of quick pictures with her phone, focusing mainly on the man Torres had called boss. As soon as she got to her computer, she would try to upload the images into the Next Generation Identification-Interstate Photo System, also known as NGI-IPS, and see if she got a hit that could help identify him.

They watched in silence as the ATV took off into the woods, Torres at the wheel and Greg on the back. Once they were out of sight, the boss man headed for the SUV. Opening the door, he paused and turned to look at the cabin. Katherine and Randy jumped away from the window, only moving again once they heard him start the vehicle and drive away.

"Well, looks like they're gone." She pushed upward, thankful her height allowed the luxury of standing in a room that had a six-foot-high ceiling, even if there was only a three-inch clearance that kept her from hitting her head. "Guess we can climb down now. We need to map out a plan, in case Torres and Greg return before Sheriff Walker."

She started to go around Randy, who had also stood but had to stay hunched over. He placed a hand on her arm, halting her. "First, I want to apologize for the things I said to you in the past." She opened her mouth to protest, and he rushed on. "It was wrong of me to make you feel like you made a bad choice. While I can't recall the details surrounding the case Chief Bradshaw was working on, I do trust you. And I'm sure your assistance that day aided in keeping Dr. Porter alive. As LEOs we must always protect the innocents who are in danger right in front of us before we worry about future victims. I'm sorry for making you think you made the wrong choice that day and for laying a guilt trip on you."

"Thank you for that. It means a lot." She took two steps in the direction of the ladder, halted and turned back to him in shock. "You just called us LEOs."

"So?"

"Do you even remember what LEO stands for?"

"Law enforcement officers. What's the—wait a minute." He gasped. "I remember my time at the academy. The classes, the instructors, the Tactical and Emergency Vehicle Operations Center and Hogan's Alley." He scooped her into a big hug, and she imagined he would have swung her around if there had been room.

His joy at some of his memory returning was evident, and Katherine instinctively embraced him back, laughing with him. She shouldn't be hugging him. He had a wife. Or an ex-wife. All she knew was that Randy either had a current wife no one knew about or he still loved his ex-wife. Why else would being married be the only memory he had when he woke up after the accident?

She gently pushed him away, a smile plastered on her face. "That's great news. Now, let's get out of here. We've got work to do if we want to stop the cartel before they stop us. Permanently."

Randy sobered, the grin on his face erased without a trace. "Okay. Let's go." He moved past her and lowered the ladder. "I'll go first."

Backing down the ladder, one rung at a time, he quickly reached the bottom and looked up. "Toss down the clothes and shoes." She did as instructed, and he caught each item, stacking them in a pile on the floor. Then he stretched out his arms and said, "Okay, your turn. Go slow and easy."

The ladder wobbled with her descent, and when she was on the third rung from the bottom, she stumbled. Randy caught her, setting her safely onto the floor.

For the second time in less than ten minutes, Randy's strong arms were wrapped around her waist, and her emotions warred with her mind. She'd promised herself to never rely on a man again. Her career was the only thing she needed to give her life meaning. Why, then, did she want to twist around in his arms and return the embrace, and bask in his strength?

Because the past twenty-four hours had been an emotional roller coaster. That's why. Katherine blinked and stepped out of Randy's arms. *Pull yourself together, girl. You're not a starry-eyed twenty-six-year-old anymore. Besides, you have a job to do that involves more lives than your own. Don't forget the people affected by the illegal dealings of the cartel. They deserve your full attention.*

She had allowed herself to get too close because of Randy's amnesia and her desire to help him. Nothing more. Once this case was over, the emotions she was feeling would subside. If they didn't, she would request a transfer.

Lightning flashed outside, followed closely by a loud rumble of thunder that shook the entire cabin. It seemed only fitting that the storm she'd seen in the distance had reached them at this precise moment, its intensity matching her current mood.

A loud boom sounded as a bolt of lightning struck a tree on the edge of the property, splitting it in two, sparks flying into the air. "Wow. That was close." Katherine turned away from the window and settled onto the couch. She'd been watching the storm out the window for the last forty-five minutes or so, the rain and lightning not showing any signs of letting up. "I wonder if Torres gave up and went home, or if he's still out there searching for us like the boss ordered."

"I've been wondering the same," Randy replied. "I wouldn't want to be caught out in this storm driving an ATV, but it would surprise me if Torres has called it quits yet."

"I agree. His normally stern demeanor seemed shaken when he was talking to the boss. I doubt he's eager to face the wrath of the one he fears by turning up without us."

"You may be right. If that's the case, they could circle back here to get out of the storm."

"That thought has crossed my mind. At least we'll have the advantage of expecting them if they show up here again." She crossed over to the kitchen and rummaged through the fridge, needing something to take her mind off the fact that there were possibly two men still in the woods in a severe thunderstorm looking to kill them. Taking sandwich meat, condiments and pickles out of the fridge, she placed them on the island beside an unopened loaf of bread and then searched through the cabinets.

A few minutes later, she carried a tray with two plates and two cups of coffee over to the sofa and set it on the coffee table. "Here, I made dinner," she said, handing one of the plates to Randy. "Just ham sandwiches and chips, but it should be filling. You still need to rebuild your strength."

He grinned. "I thought my strength was pretty good when I pulled the stairs upward into the attic using my belt."

The bruise on the side of his face had started to fade, and his complexion didn't seem as peaked as it had at the hospital. Wow. Twenty-four hours ago, they had been in Randy's hospital room, him sleeping and her trying to figure out how to handle his amnesia. It seemed so much longer. Guess time slowed down when one was on the run for their life. "How much of that strength was simply adrenaline? You're still recovering from your accident. Now, eat."

"Yes, ma'am," he said in a joking manner. Picking up half of one of the sandwiches, he took a big bite. His eyes widened, and he chewed with gusto, obvious enjoyment on his face. Ham and cheese with lots of mustard and a little mayonnaise. The way she had seen him make his sandwiches in the past. Randy swallowed. "You make a very good sandwich."

"I'm glad you like it."

He looked at her, his brow furrowed. "Doesn't it seem strange that there's so much food here, in a cabin that's only used seasonally?"

"Possibly. But I checked all the dates on the milk and things in the fridge, and most don't expire for two weeks." She plucked a napkin off the tray and wiped her mouth. "I noticed the rods and things you got out earlier were for fly-fishing, which is really popular in this area during the spring. When you take all of that into consideration, it's plausible the sheriff was here last weekend to fish and stored up enough supplies so he wouldn't have to bring groceries every time he came."

"Sounds reasonable." He leaned forward, scrutinizing her as he asked, "But do you trust him? Is it possible he's working with the cartel, and he's the reason they were able to follow us here?"

"Trust him? Yes, but with a healthy dose of suspicion and caution." She laughed, realizing how that must sound. Was it possible to trust and be suspicious at the same time? "I never trust anyone completely. Wanda seems to trust him, so I choose to have confidence in her knowledge of him. Until he does something to prove I shouldn't. Also, while I wonder if he may be hiding something from us, I don't think he's in with the cartel." She took a sip of coffee. The caffeine would keep her up half the night, but the warmth it provided helped ward off the chill that had settled around the cabin when the rain started. "If he wanted us dead, why not kill us himself last night?"

Seeming to ponder her question, he popped the last bite of sandwich into his mouth and chewed, not answering.

While she wanted him to validate her theory, she also knew, if Sheriff Walker wanted them dead, he may have turned them over to the cartel's hit men to keep his hands clean and not have their deaths traced back to him. *Stop that. Wanda believes he's one of the good guys. Trust her instincts.*

Randy closed his eyes and rubbed his temples. He hadn't complained of a headache today, but she guessed it was too much to hope the migraines would have simply disappeared.

"Do you need a pain reliever?" When he

didn't reply, she started to stand. "Here, let me get—"

He grasped her hand, stopping her. "No. It's okay. Just a dull ache. Nothing bad." He tried to give her a reassuring smile, but the pain she saw in his eyes gave him away.

"You don't have to try and be tough, you know."

"If it gets worse, I'll take something. But for now, it's fine."

Katherine nodded. "Okay. I'll just take care of the dishes." She pulled her hand free of his, scooped up the plates and crossed to the kitchen, thankful there was still enough daylight streaming through the windows to help her see as she washed the dishes.

"Speaking of the sheriff. Shouldn't he be back by now?"

She had been thinking the same thing. "Any number of things could have delayed him. For one, the heavy rainfall could have caused mudslides, blocking the road. We may need to be prepared in case he doesn't return tonight."

The storm raging outside wasn't letting up, the cloud cover casting a dark shadow that would soon turn into a pitch-black, moonless night. And with Torres and Greg looming somewhere in the dark, the lights inside the cabin would need to remain off. At least they'd be warm. The sheriff said the central heat unit stayed on a cool sixty degrees when he wasn't in residence. As long as they kept the lights off and didn't bump the thermostat up where the unit ran nonstop, they shouldn't attract attention if Torres and Greg returned.

Lightning flashed and an explosion sounded in the front yard. Randy rushed over, and they watched through the kitchen window as sparks and smoke spewed from the transformer at the edge of the drive. Glancing at the stove, she noted the clock face was blank. Katherine reached for the light switch and flipped it up and down twice. No power. Now they'd also be without heat. Because even though there was a fireplace with wood stacked beside it at the ready, they wouldn't be able to light it for fear of giving themselves away.

Randy shivered and rubbed his arms. He had pulled the sweatshirt he'd taken from the hospital on over his other clothes earlier, but the cold still seeped into his body. The electricity had been out for almost ten hours, and the temps had probably dropped twenty degrees since nightfall.

And they couldn't build a fire—sending up smoke signals to let the cartel or anyone else know they were in fact in the sheriff's cabin. So, no heat.

Not only was he cold, but his legs and back ached. Of course, that was his own fault for sleeping in the oversize chair instead of going to the bedroom he had slept in the night before. But he had wanted to stay close in case Torres and Greg had shown up while Katherine stood watch the first half of the night.

He smiled. His partner was one stubborn woman. She'd still be standing guard if he hadn't woken up an hour ago and insisted it was his turn. Glancing toward the couch, he could barely make out the shape of her body curled up, sleeping. Randy needed to stretch. He stood and reached his arms above his head, trying to work the kinks out of his back muscles.

Thankful the clouds had passed and a big, bright moon now hung in the sky, he used the faint light that peeked in through the shades to guide his steps to the back of the cabin. Going into each of the bedrooms, he pulled the comforters off the beds and returned to the living room. He covered Katherine with one and then settled back into his own chair with the other.

Surely, it couldn't be more than a few hours until sunrise. Would the sheriff show up once it was daylight? No matter. Randy had already decided they had to find a way out of the remote area and get to their computer at the safe house, even if it meant hiking to town for a ride. They couldn't waste any more time. He needed to search for answers to recover his lost memories, and they had to piece together the information they'd gathered and finally shut down the cartel. Time was wasting. No matter what, with or without Sheriff Walker's return, they would leave the cabin at first light.

Idly, he traced the crystal on his broken watch and wished he knew what time it was. Katherine had placed her cell phone on the coffee table earlier. Was it still there? With an outstretched arm, he lightly patted the solid oak table, stretching and searching. Finally, his hand made contact with the cool metal case.

Clutching the phone to his chest, he settled back into the comfort of the chair and pulled the cover over his head. Couldn't allow the light from the screen to show in case Torres and Greg were still out there somewhere looking in. It might seem a little drastic, but he didn't feel like he could be too cautious.

He tapped the phone screen, blinking at its brightness. 3:57 a.m. Three hours until sunup. Hmm. Did the cell phone have internet data? If so, maybe he could start searching for James and Martha. He swiped a finger upward. A keypad appeared on the screen. Ugh. It was hopeless. If he couldn't remember his life history, how was he supposed to remember Katherine's cell phone password. If he'd ever known it to begin with.

"What are you doing?"

He jumped at the sound of Katherine's voice and dropped the cell phone. Flailing his arms, he pulled the cover from over his head. "I… um…was checking the time. On your phone. And, uh, I thought I might try to do some research. You know, for answers to my background. Only—"

"It's password protected," she said before he could.

He stood and shook the blanket. The phone clattered to the floor. He picked it up and handed it to her. "I'm sorry. I shouldn't have messed with your phone without permission. I really did just want to check the time, at first anyway."

She pressed the button on the side of the device to make it go to sleep and slipped it into her back pocket. "It's okay. I know you're anxious to find out whatever you can. But, I'm afraid, even if you would have known my password, you wouldn't have been able to do much research. Since we're undercover, we're using basic phones that more or less are only good for text messages and calls."

"Yeah, I'm not surprised." He struggled to keep the disappointment out of his voice. "As much as I hate the idea of waiting, I'm beginning to think I need to put my own, personal struggles aside until after we've solved this case."

"I promise to help you find answers, no matter how long it takes."

Suddenly, he wanted to know more about her life. He'd never even thought that she might actually be married to someone other than him. But the Bureau couldn't be her entire life.

A light swept across the room. Headlights. Someone was coming up the drive very slowly.

Katherine palmed her revolver and moved toward the door. "I'm not hiding this time."

He tried not to bristle at her words. He wasn't a hang-back-and-hide kind of person. She had to know that. "Agreed. No hiding. We have a better idea what we're up against this time." His palm itched for his service weapon.

What could he use in place of his revolver for self-defense? A knife. He'd replaced the one he'd taken out of the drawer earlier. This time, he'd selected a bigger one.

Thump. His shin connected with the coffee table. He clenched his jaw, forcing down the exclamation that had sprung to his lips. The moon had moved behind a cloud, no longer providing much light. How had Katherine walked across the room in the dark with ease?

"A foot to your left," Katherine whispered. "Then it's a clear path to the island."

"How are you doing that?"

"I have excellent night vision." She laughed. "And I memorized the floor plan after the power went out." Another reason to be thankful she was his partner.

Knife in hand, he moved to the front window and peered between the slats in the blind. If the person coming up the drive was a foe, they would be in for a fight.

EIGHT

Randy's heart pounded, protective instincts surging through his body. He wanted to swap places with Katherine. Stand in front of her. Protect her from the danger that threatened to charge through the door. He doubted she would be happy with him if he did any of those things. Besides, she had the gun, not him.

She was also a highly skilled agent. He trusted her with his life. Although, he really did need to remedy his lack of gun situation. Fast.

"It's an SUV. Not a pickup truck. They've stopped." Katherine gave a play-by-play, even though he was also watching the scene unfold. "Okay, get ready."

A car door slammed, and Randy sucked in his breath. The silhouette of the driver rounded the front of the SUV, the beam from the slowly dimming automatic headlights illuminating his face. Sheriff Walker. The headlights went dark as he jogged toward the cabin.

The air whooshed out of Randy's lungs, carrying a fraction of the tension from the day with it. He heard the click of the door lock being disengaged and the knob turning. "Wait. Don't open it until he gets closer."

"I'm not a rookie."

Randy hadn't meant to insult her. Before he could apologize, the sheriff's footsteps pounded on the porch. When he drew closer, Katherine opened the door, pulled him inside, closed the door and locked it.

"What's going on?" a startled Sheriff Walker demanded.

"We could ask you the same thing." Randy moved to stand beside Katherine. "What took you so long getting back here?"

"Multiple things. Including filling out paperwork, looking over the Jeep that was towed after being abandoned on the interstate last night, trying to find clues—" He paused. The sound of a light switch being flipped not once, but twice, echoed in the silence. "The power's out? It's cold in here. Why didn't you build a fire?"

"Because we had visitors earlier. And we didn't want to run the risk of them returning." Katherine holstered her weapon.

"Bathroom. Now," the sheriff commanded, taking off down the hall. There was a thud. "Ow. What? Why are the attic steps down?"

"We'll explain. Press against the wall. It's easy to get around them." Katherine took the lead.

"Sorry." Randy grasped the ladder and pushed it upward before continuing on to the bathroom. "I left them down in case we needed to go back up there."

Once they were all safely inside the windowless bathroom with the door closed, Katherine used her cell phone to provide light.

The sheriff reached into the cabinet under the sink and pulled out two candles, then opened the drawer and retrieved a lighter. Soon, light and a sweet honeysuckle scent filled the room. Randy smiled, cocking an eyebrow at the older law enforcement officer.

Sheriff Walker grunted. "My wife insists on bringing these things up here when she comes with me for a weekend. Now, tell me about the visitors."

They quickly told the older lawman about the goons showing up, hiding in the attic and overhearing the boss man's orders for Torres and Greg to stay out in the woods all night, if that's what it took to find Randy and Katherine.

"Hiding in the attic was smart thinking."

"Thanks," Randy said, "but now you see why we couldn't build a fire."

"Do you really think they're still out in the woods watching the cabin?" Sheriff Walker rubbed his chin. "I can't imagine anyone staying out in the thunderstorms that passed through. The lightning was bad, but the rain was torrential. Another reason I was late was because a mudslide blocked the entire road about five miles south of here. I had to turn around and take a longer route, going southwest and then circling back on a different road. Fortunately, it was clear even though it's a less-traveled road."

"All the same. The boss didn't sound like someone Torres would want to cross."

"She's right. Even if the thunderstorms made them give up the search, the rain stopped hours ago. They could have resumed their hunt by now."

"Okay, so we keep you two hidden. Then in the morning, I sneak you out of here. But I think we'd be fine building a fire and warming up."

Randy opened his mouth to protest, but the sheriff rushed on. "I come up here almost every weekend from early March through

September. It's Saturday. It would seem out of place for me to be here and not light a fire."

"I don't know." Randy looked at Katherine. Her expression mimicked his concern.

"I tell you what." Sheriff Walker pulled a manila file folder from inside his denim jacket and handed it to Katherine. "Here's the file I wanted us to go over. You guys decide if you want to let me build a fire so you can thaw out, or not. In the meantime, I'm going to run back out to my patrol car and grab the tennis shoes I borrowed from my wife for you." He eyed her bare feet. "I hope you wear a size seven and a half." He turned and left before either of them could say another word.

"That was thoughtful of him to bring you shoes."

"Yes, but I still don't think it's wise to build a fire. Do you?"

"No. Not really. If Torres and Greg return, they'll see the sheriff's vehicle and might not think anything of it. But there's no need to draw them back in this direction with smoke. Besides, if we leave at sunrise, we'll only be here—" The thunderous roar of an ATV interrupted Randy.

"They're back!" they said in unison.

Bolting from the room, Randy raced toward the front of the cabin, Katherine close behind him. They stood on either side of the front window and watched as an ATV with two riders rounded the house. A gunshot ringing out. Sheriff Walker clutched his left shoulder and fell to the ground beside his SUV.

Gun in hand, Katherine stepped into the shadow of the porch. Bracing against a corner post, she took aim at the ATV.

"Cover me. I'm going to check on Sheriff Walker," Randy said from behind her.

"Go!" she urged in a hushed tone as he took off down the steps.

The ATV turned toward the cabin, its lights flashing across the porch. She pulled the trigger. One. Two. Three shots in rapid succession. An exclamation of pain followed. She'd hit one of them.

Katherine took aim again. Before she could get off another shot, the ATV did a U-turn. The passenger on the back fell off as the driver sped away.

She eased off the porch. One step at a time. Her eyes stayed on the dark form lying in the clearing just beyond the drive. Pausing by the sheriff's patrol vehicle, she assessed the situation. The sheriff was on the ground. Randy had slipped his sweatshirt off and was pressing it over the wound. "How is he?"

"I can't tell if the bullet hit a major artery. He's lost a good deal of blood."

"I'm okay." Sheriff Walker coughed. "Need more than a bullet to the shoulder to take me out."

"He needs an ambulance. Hold this." Randy nodded toward the bloodstained sweatshirt.

She knelt and applied pressure. Randy opened the door of the SUV and crawled inside. A few seconds later she heard him on the radio giving the code for officer down. His training had kicked in again.

"Sir, I need the address for dispatch." Katherine leaned close, getting the information to pass on.

Soon Randy was on the ground beside her. "Help's on the way."

"I need to check on the guy I shot."

"Put those shoes on first." Randy pointed to a pair of white tennis shoes on the ground beside the sheriff. The ones Sheriff Walker had gone to the vehicle to retrieve for her.

If he hadn't left the safety of the cabin, he wouldn't have been shot. Tears burned the backs of her eyes as she slipped her feet into the shoes. Perfect fit.

"Be careful," Randy whispered as she stood.

"Will do." She peered over the hood of the SUV. The body hadn't moved. Every muscle on high alert, she slowly crossed the yard, eyes focused on the victim and ears tuned to hear the return of the ATV.

Reaching the body, she knelt and placed two fingers on the neck. No pulse. Pulling her phone out of her back pocket, she turned on the flashlight feature and rolled the body over. Greg. It figured that Torres would run and leave his buddy's body behind.

She returned to Randy and the sheriff. "Torres's sidekick Greg is dead."

Randy looked up. "How much time do you think we have before Torres returns with reinforcements?"

"I don't know. Depends on how far away they are. Did dispatch tell you how long it would take the police and an ambulance to arrive?"

"ETA was fifteen minutes, or longer because of the mudslide."

The sheriff coughed. "We're in the middle of nowhere. Look. You guys need to go."

"We can't leave you." The suggestion horrified Katherine.

"You can, and you will, missy." The older officer covered her hand with his cold, bloody one. "You're close to solving this case. Sticking around to give a report and fill out paperwork will delay your investigation. What's stopping this group from picking up and moving again? Isn't that their MO?"

"He's right," Randy chimed in. "Go, get both of the comforters. I'll use the sleeves to fasten the sweatshirt so it continues to apply pressure. We'll make him as comfortable as we can, and then we're out of here."

"But—"

"You're wasting…time," Sheriff Walker said breathlessly.

"And how are we supposed to get out of here? On foot? We can't very well go driving around in your police vehicle, especially after you've been shot."

"There's a cabin about a mile through the woods. Belongs to a friend from California. I oversee things when he's not here. You'll find a key chain—with a red-and-white bobber— on a peg by the refrigerator. It has keys to the cabin and to the old pickup truck he keeps here." Sheriff Walker closed his eyes. "Now, go. I'm tired."

She looked to Randy, and he jerked his head toward the cabin.

Katherine took off at a run. Once inside, she turned on the phone's flashlight. No need to worry about being seen any longer. She located the key chain and shoved it into her front pocket. Then she went to the bathroom and gathered the file that she'd dropped when they heard the ATV and tucked it into her waistband. Finally, she grabbed the comforters and made her way outside.

"I got everything. How is he?"

"Weak. He passed out after he gave me directions to his friend's cabin." Randy took the comforters and draped them across the sheriff, tucking them in around him to trap as much heat as possible. "His heartbeat's faint, but steady."

"I hate leaving before help arrives."

"I know. But we have to trust God to watch over him."

She resisted the urge to roll her eyes. Even with amnesia, Randy was touting the virtues of God. She'd never had his faith and doubted she ever would.

The distant sound of a siren reached her ears. They could go. Help had arrived. Five minutes ahead of schedule, most likely because of the call of an officer down.

"That's our signal. Let's go." Randy clasped his hand around hers, and they raced toward the woods.

NINE

Follow the stream. The terrain will become difficult as you navigate down the mountainside. When you hear the waterfall, start looking for the swinging bridge. Cross the bridge and follow the trail to the clearing. You'll see a small two-story cabin. The truck is parked in the attached carport. Randy replayed the sheriff's instructions in his mind as they ran away from the scene behind them.

They reached the stream and ducked into a small thicket of trees. The sirens drew closer, and he saw the flashing lights of the emergency vehicles as they wove their way up the long drive.

"Please, Lord, let Sheriff Walker be okay and help us reach safety," he prayed, finding comfort in speaking the words aloud.

"You always do that," Katherine stated.

"Pray?"

"Yes, out loud. Usually, when we're facing a challenge."

Even though her words were stated as a matter-of-fact, Randy had a feeling she'd meant them negatively. "Well, I would say we're definitely facing a challenge. Let's get moving before the responding officers get out of their vehicles and decide to search the area."

"Which way?"

"Downstream." He took the lead, staying close to the tree line in an effort to hide their movements until they were out of sight of the cabin.

They inched their way from tree to tree, using their feet to search for rocks, tree roots or other things they could trip over, much like a blind person would use their hands to see. Each step was a struggle as the mud pulled at their shoes, slowing them down even further.

Ten minutes into their hike, they had put enough distance between themselves and the sheriff's cabin that Randy felt safe enough to step away from the shadow of the trees. Walking on the rocks that bordered the water enabled them to speed up. The moon, sinking lower in the sky, cast a little light that helped them see tripping hazards.

"Do you think the sheriff's going to be okay, because you asked God to make it so?" Katherine's question wasn't accusatory or confrontational, but he sensed she had been let down by someone in the past and God had received the blame for it.

"Don't you believe in God and His love?"

They continued on in silence. He thought she wasn't going to answer, but then she confessed, "I used to. My family started attending church when I was nine, and I became a Christian at twelve. That was before I learned God doesn't answer prayers."

Randy sent up a silent prayer that he would choose the right words so he could be an encouragement to her, not a stumbling block. "I hope the sheriff will be okay. And I think he will be. However, if he isn't, it won't be God's fault."

"You asked Him to save the sheriff. If He doesn't, why wouldn't it be His fault?" She sighed. "I'm sorry. I didn't mean to sound disrespectful. I am interested in your answer."

"The evil that exists in this world is responsible for the sheriff getting shot, not God."

"And if we make it through this, it will be because *we* did our jobs, not because of some higher power," she said in a whisper that he was sure she hadn't intended for him to hear.

Let her think what she wanted. He wouldn't push his beliefs on anyone, even though it saddened him that she didn't understand the glory of God. *Lord, I pray that Katherine's heart will be softened so she can find her way back to You.*

The roar of water reached his ears. "Do you hear that? It's the waterfall the sheriff mentioned. We must be getting close to the swinging bridge."

Dawn was emerging, and the darkness had become more of a dark gray than an inky black. He estimated they had about twenty minutes before streaks of sunrise brightened the sky. "We need to pick up the pace. If the sheriff has remained unconscious, there's a good chance the responding officers called in a K-9 unit to search the woods for additional suspects."

"Once we find the bridge, how much farther is it?"

"All he said was 'cross the bridge and follow the trail to the clearing.' There will be a two-story cabin, and we'll find the truck parked in the carport. I got the impression it wasn't too far from the bridge."

A little while later, Katherine exclaimed, "Look! There's a rope tied around that tree." She pointed at a pine tree. It stood at least forty feet tall with thick underbrush around its base, hiding the bottom eight or nine feet of its trunk, a thick rope barely visible through the vines. "And is that the bridge?"

The tree in question was a couple of yards ahead, where the stream curved to the right. There was a definite outline of a rope bridge running diagonally across the stream, suspended about five feet above the water. "Good eyes! I can barely make that out from here."

They hurried to the tree, and Katherine pulled out her cell phone, using it to shine light on the area. The tree was covered in vines, making it difficult to get to the bridge.

"The only way we're going to be able to reach it is to go around the tree and approach from the water."

"That's going to be tricky. The rapids are so much stronger here. I don't see the waterfall, but from the sound, it's got to be close."

"Agreed. Follow me." He grabbed onto one of the vines and pulled with all his strength. It held strong. *Lord, I pray this works.*

While keeping his grip on the vine, he fought his way through the underbrush and went around the tree on the left side. Halfway around the trunk, he felt Katherine grab hold of his shirt. "Not so fast. I'm getting tangled in the weeds."

Randy slowed his steps and stopped when he reached the water's edge. There was a wooden platform attached to the tree, but the vines had swallowed the steps leading up to it. This gave him pause for concern. How long had it been since anyone had crossed this bridge? He turned to check on Katherine. "Are you okay?"

She nodded. "Yes."

"Hang on to this vine and don't let go. I'm going to try and pull myself up on the platform." He searched her eyes, but only saw sheer determination. Once again, he was thankful to have her as a partner. He imagined they must have always worked well together.

Leaning as far as he could while maintaining his hold on the tree, he reached for the rope attached to the platform. His fingers barely grazed it. He tried again, this time leaning too far from the tree, losing his balance and swaying over the water. Katherine grasped his shirttail and pulled, allowing him to lunge toward the tree and regain his balance.

Hugging the trunk, he took several deep breaths and willed his heart to return to a normal rhythm.

"Are you okay?"

"Yeah. Now, let's do this."

He took a deep breath and stepped off the bank, praying he would be able to keep his grip on the vine if he lost his footing. If not, the rapids would push him over the waterfall, which would surely result in his death. Icy-cold water ran over his shoes in waves that soaked his pant legs up to his knees. Maintaining his grip on the vine, he waded closer to the platform. Reaching the solid wooden post that held the platform above the water, he released his hold on the vine, wrapped both arms as high as he could around the post and jumped. He hooked his legs around the pillar and shimmied up it.

Once he reached the top, he swung his leg over the handrail and jumped down onto the platform, landing in a crouched position. Thankfully, it didn't give way with his weight. He hoped this meant the boards that composed the actual bridge part were still solid, too. He pushed back into a seated position and spun around to talk Katherine through copying his movements. When she reached the pillar, he grasped her forearms and lifted her to the platform.

"Thanks," she said, her teeth chattering.

"Let's get moving. We'll warm up once we're in the truck."

The first rays of the sunrise crested over the mountain, sending streaks of orange, yellow and purple into the sky. Thankful for the additional light, he started across the bridge. Surprisingly, it was more stable than one might have suspected, given the overgrown condition

of the steps leading to it. Other than having
to stretch to step across a few broken boards,
the crossing was uneventful. That was until
they reached the shore on the other side of the
stream.

As soon as they stepped onto solid ground,
the sound of dogs barking and handlers yelling orders reached them. He scanned the area
they had come from but didn't see anything.
By the sound of the K-9, he knew they and
their handlers weren't far behind.

Katherine froze, and the hair at the nape of
her neck stood on end as goose bumps formed.
The sound of the dogs hunting them drew
closer. She had never imagined being hunted
by law enforcement one day. "Which way?"

"There." Randy pointed to a barely visible
trail, and they raced toward it.

Katherine wondered how many years it had
been since Sheriff Walker had visited this side
of the stream or seen the swinging bridge. She
ignored the sting of briars and branches cutting her face and arms as she ran through the
woods. The only advantage they had was the
overgrown steps at the swinging bridge separating them from the K-9. As difficult as it
had been for her and Randy to fight their way
through the foliage and onto the bridge, she

could only imagine the struggle for the handlers with their K-9.

Sunlight up ahead told her they were almost to a clearing. The cabin had to be close. She jumped over a fallen log, with Randy right behind her.

They burst into the clearing. A two-story cabin stood twenty yards away, an older-model blue-and-white Ford truck parked under the carport awning. In one last final sprint, they reached the truck, Randy two steps ahead of her.

He opened the driver's side door, turned and held out his hand. "Give me the keys."

"Nothing doing." She shook her head. "You lost your identification in the accident. If we get stopped for any reason by a police officer, it'll be more difficult to talk our way out of trouble if you're driving."

"But it's a manual transmission. Do you know how to drive a stick?"

"I do. Do you?"

"I'm pretty sure I do."

"That's not good enough. Now get in." She ducked under his arm and slipped behind the wheel, pulling the folder the sheriff had given them out of her waistband and tossing it on the dashboard.

To his credit, Randy didn't argue. He jogged

around the front of the vehicle, opened the passenger door and pushed a wide-brim fishing hat and vest off the seat.

She started the truck, and he reached over to turn on the heat. Then he pulled a handgun out of his waistband and settled it on his lap.

"Where'd you get that?"

"Sheriff Walker told me to take it. It's his personal gun." He slapped the dashboard. "Now go."

The carport was open on both ends. Katherine put the truck into first gear, pulled forward and circled the house. She spared a quick glance at the woods. There was no sign of the K-9 or their handlers. Accelerating, she headed down the drive, thankful she didn't grind any of the gears.

"I'm impressed. You're really good driving a manual transmission."

"My momma taught me. She said there were three things concerning a car that every driver should always know how to do…change a tire, check the oil and drive a manual transmission."

"Sounds like an interesting woman."

Katherine felt his gaze on her as they bounced over the rutted-out drive. Her mom was remarkable, burying a son and then raising two daughters alone after their dad left them. Since his statement didn't require a response, she focused on driving. She wasn't in the habit of discussing her personal family life with her coworkers, and she had no desire to start now.

Reaching the road, she turned north. Katherine had no idea where they were exactly, but Wyoming was north of Colorado. Also, the sheriff had said there was a mudslide to the south. While she suspected that had been a different road, she couldn't take the chance.

"Do you have any idea where you're going?"

"Not really, but we need to get to the safe house in Wyoming. So, if we head north, at least we're going in the right direction."

"Sounds logical."

Randy rifled through the glove compartment.

"Yes!" he exclaimed. "You've got to love people who still believe in paper maps and don't just rely on electronics." He held up a Colorado map, yellowed with age.

"That's all well and good, but don't you kind of need to know where we are before you can map out where we're going?"

He placed the gun into the glove compartment and pulled out an old owner's manual. Flipping through the pages, he turned and smiled at her triumphantly. "Owner's registration and insurance. Complete with address."

The map made a crinkly sound, like walking on dried leaves, as he opened it. A section of the map blocked her view of the road, and she pushed it away. "Sorry," he mumbled without looking up, intent on finding their location. In the meantime, Katherine would be on the lookout for a gas station or convenience store. Local folks were usually excellent resources for directions.

They drove in silence for the next few miles. The sun had risen, its warmth engulfing the cab of the truck. A pins-and-needles sensation in her feet alerted her that they were beginning to warm up from their unexpected dip into the icy cold water. No wonder people wore waders when they fished in a stream.

"Do you want to go backroads or interstate?" Randy asked, his finger tracing a line on the map.

"I want whichever route will get me out of the mountains and on flatter ground." She slowed her speed as she took a sharp curve, recalling the reason the sheriff was delayed last night. *Please, don't let there be a mudslide.* The prayer went up before she even registered what she was doing. How many times had she prayed in the last two days? She'd lost count. Oh, well, God may or may not be listening, but it couldn't hurt to try. *Lord, I don't expect You to answer my prayers, but please answer Randy's.*

TEN

Tick. Tick. Tick. What was that sound? Randy furrowed his brow. *Had someone planted a bomb in his vehicle, like they had in Trevor's? He had to do something. It was raining hard, and he was traveling up a curvy mountain road. There was no place to pull off.*

"Are you okay? Randy?" Katherine's voice sounded as if it were coming from inside a long tunnel. "Can you hear me?" Someone shook his arm, punctuating the urgency in her voice. "Okay, you're scaring me."

He fought to open his eyes. What was wrong with him? His eyelids felt like one-hundred-pound weights. *Tick. Tick. Tick.* He jerked upward. Fully awake and alert. "Where are we?"

Randy looked around. At some point while he slept, she had stopped at a convenience-store-gas-station combo named Joni's Gas 'n Go.

"Wyoming. By my best estimate, we're about

thirty-five minutes from the safe house." She sat sideways in the driver's seat, watching him. "I'm surprised I didn't wake you when I got out and pumped gas. I would have let you sleep, but you seemed in distress."

He had only intended to close his eyes for a few minutes. Just long enough to allow the headache to pass. Randy massaged his temples. The familiar dull ache had settled behind his eyes. "How long was I asleep?"

"Not long. Twenty minutes." Katherine leaned closer. "How's the headache?"

"Better. A dull ache." Sunlight streamed through the window, and he squinted. "Sunglasses would be nice."

Katherine smiled. "I think I can do something about that," she said, opening the truck door. "I'll be right back." The door clicked closed, and he winced.

He watched as she crossed the parking lot and entered the convenience store. A garbage truck roared by on the highway. A school bus stopped to pick up kids standing in front of a house across the street. Every sound seemed magnified. *Tick. Tick. Tick.* Where was that sound coming from? His watch. He bent his arm and put it to his ear. A smile split his face. It was working again.

The time wasn't accurate, but the seconds

hand bobbed around the dial. He spotted a bank halfway down the block. The digital sign out front proclaimed the temperature was forty-two degrees, and the time was 7:13 a.m.

Grasping the crown, he pulled it out and started turning it. The hands on the clock flew around the face as he wound it, until finally the time was correct. He pushed the crown back in and bent his arm to listen again.

The driver's side door opened, and Katherine slid into the vehicle. "What are you doing?"

He smiled. "My watch is working. I'll need to take it to a repair shop to have the crystal replaced, but at least it wasn't destroyed like I originally feared."

"That is good news. I know how much that watch means to you." She handed him a plastic shopping bag that was heavier than one would expect for a pair of sunglasses. "I hope these will do. They didn't have a wide selection."

Randy pulled out the sunglasses—basic aviator style with silver metal frames and dark lenses—and slipped them on. "These are great. Thanks. But what else is in here?" He pulled out a cell phone, flipping it over in his hands.

"It's a prepaid phone. I want to call Wanda after we get to the safe house."

"Why can't you use the cell phone issued by the Bureau?"

She started the truck and backed out of the parking space. "I could, but it doesn't hurt to have an extra layer of security."

Why would she need more security than a Bureau-issued phone would provide? He rapped his fingers on his knee, his mind assessing the situation. "You think someone has hacked your phone?"

"What? No." She shook her head and shifted into the next gear. "Well, not the way I think you mean. I don't think it's being tracked or anything..."

"But?"

Katherine sighed. "Wanda thinks there may be a mole in the Bureau."

"A mole?" He shoved his hand through his hair, picturing the people he had worked with for many years. All hardworking law enforcement officers dedicated to putting criminals behind bars. "That's ridiculous. I can't think of a single person in the Bureau who would work for the cartel."

She looked at him with a shocked expression before quickly returning her attention to the road. "You remember your coworkers?"

It took a few moments for him to process her words. What was the big deal? Then it hit him. His memories had returned. The ones involving his career anyway. He still couldn't recall

his wife—ex-wife, according to Katherine—
or what happened to their relationship.

"Randy?"

He jerked his head in her direction. "Yes. I
think I do. At least, most of my memories concerning my career have returned."

"Tell me who or what you remember. Maybe
discussing things will help us figure out what
we're missing."

"That's a good idea." He dug back into the
convenience store bag and pulled out the other
two items he'd seen in there earlier—a small
notepad and a pen. "Thanks for this," he said
as he clicked the pen.

She smiled. "Of course."

It seemed that she knew him very well.
Randy felt at a disadvantage because, even
though he remembered his coworkers from
the Bureau, he didn't remember working with
Katherine. "I must confess, I still don't recall
the case we're working on."

"Try not to stress too much." She slowed to
a stop at a four-way intersection and turned
left. "It seems like your memories are returning as you need them, mostly when you aren't
trying too hard."

"True. Okay, so let's get to work. Who at the
Bureau could be the mole?" They proceeded
to work through the list of their coworkers,

starting with Wanda Richardson and working their way through the field agents, secretaries, IT crew and even the janitorial staff. When they had finished, Randy had filled eight pages in the notebook. Every person on the list had proved their loyalties. He couldn't imagine any of them turning rogue.

"Have we forgotten anyone?"

"Not that I can think of." He tapped the pen against the notebook. "Well, except for you and me."

"You think I'm the mole?"

"I didn't say that."

"Then are you saying you are?"

"Of course not."

"Okay, then I think we can leave ourselves off the list."

He drew in a slow, deep breath, counted to ten and released it. "I'm sorry. I didn't mean to imply that I thought you were the mole. It's just I don't really know anything about you, outside of the fact that we have worked together for almost a year. And that's fuzzy. Ugh." He balled his fist. "Why can't I remember the case?"

"We're about twenty minutes from the safe house. Do you want to spend the rest of the time reviewing the case?"

"I think I'd rather wait until we get to your computer and I can look over our files. That way I'll have all the data." He put away the notepad and pen and turned toward her. "In the meantime, I'd like to get to know you. Your past. What made you become an agent? And your family... Are you married?"

As soon as he voiced the question, she visibly stiffened, and her grip tightened on the steering wheel. Interesting. She was hiding something. And he intended to find out what it was.

The silence in the truck's cab felt like a coiled rattlesnake, ready to strike at any moment. Katherine missed the old Randy. The one who did his job and remained aloof, not interested in being friends. No, that wasn't true. There were things to like about his new persona. She actually felt more like a partner and less like an underling. For the first time in eleven months, she had taken the lead in dangerous situations and not just sat back taking orders. She really didn't want that to change now that his memory had started to return. But was the feeling of camaraderie worth disclosing personal details of her past?

"I'm sorry." She jumped at the sound of Randy's voice. "I didn't realize my questions would be so difficult for you to answer. We can move on to another topic."

"No, it's okay. I'll answer the simple question first." Katherine swallowed, pushing her pride past the lump in her throat, and moistened her lips. Here goes nothing. "I decided to become a law enforcement officer when I was in the seventh grade. The year my brother, who was a junior in college, died from a drug overdose."

"That must have been a horrible experience for your family."

"It was an eight-year ordeal for my parents, but they kept it from the rest of us. He battled drugs from the time he was fourteen. Our parents sent him to rehab twice, wiping out their savings to save their only son. For the longest time, I didn't know Jimmy was using drugs. My parents just said he was sick. He was so gaunt, his face sunken in and his hair falling out. I thought he had cancer."

Randy reached over and squeezed her hand. Tears burned the back of her eyes at his nonjudgmental compassion. Anger at her brother that she thought she'd suppressed long ago threatened to bubble to the surface. In his selfishness, Jimmy had robbed her family of everything. Not just monetary things, but love and happiness, too. "Five years into the battle, it finally seemed that he'd beaten his addiction.

He got his GED and completed two years at a local community college."

"Then what happened?"

"He wanted more independence, so he applied to a school out of state. He convinced our mom and dad it would be okay. This was the next logical step in his complete recovery, or so he said." She activated the blinker and slowed to make the turn into the parking lot of a popular chain grocery store. If they were going to hole up at the safe house for a few days, they'd need supplies. "Before the first semester was halfway over, my dad got a call from the college telling him Jimmy had overdosed and had been rushed to the hospital. My parents got on the first flight out. When they reached the hospital, Jimmy was hooked up to all kinds of machines. They were told the overdose caused him to have a seizure that cut off the oxygen to his brain. He was brain-dead."

"I'm so—"

"Don't. Please. Don't say you're sorry. I've had enough sorries to last a lifetime." As soon as the words came out, she wished she could snatch them back. It wasn't his fault all the neighbors and school teachers and principals had looked at her family with pity.

There was an empty parking spot close to the entrance. She pulled into it and cut off the engine. Turning toward Randy, she offered him a smile, her lip trembling. "I appreciate the sentiment. Really, I do. It's okay to want to sympathize with me, but *sorry* won't bring Jimmy back or change the things that happened to my family. What I need more than 'I'm sorry' is your help to get as many drug dealers off the streets as we can. Because that will change the outcome for other families."

"Definitely. We'll start with the León Dormido Cartel. But we won't stop with them."

His smile sent her heart soaring. Confidence radiated off him like heat radiating off a sidewalk in Arizona on a summer day, and she believed he could achieve all that he promised.

Randy sat in the truck in the grocery store parking lot. He had thought about going in with Katherine to get supplies but decided it might be best to give her some time alone with her thoughts. Nothing he could have said would have eased the pain he had seen in her eyes. Losing a family member to drugs was a horrible thing to go through. Although he'd never experienced such a tragedy firsthand, he had spent enough time in law enforcement to know the devastation that occurred when drugs were involved in the untimely death of a loved one. He fully intended to keep his promise, too. First, they would capture the men behind the León Dormido Cartel, then they would move on to the next drug ring. One by one, he would help her remove as many illegal drugs as he could from the streets.

Before she told him the story of her brother, Katherine had said she would start with the simple question first. Curiosity made him wonder why she hadn't answered his question about being married. The sheer fact that she'd avoided that question made him sure she wasn't. Maybe she had been, once, but it hadn't worked out. He couldn't imagine anything being harder to answer than what she'd already shared with him. Oh, well, she'd talk when she was ready. In the meantime, he needed to focus on the task at hand.

He reached for the folder the sheriff had given them and froze. The sun glinted off his watch. *"It's a World War II A-11 military watch. It belonged to my great-grandfather. My mom gave it to my dad on their wedding day. After Dad died, it was kept in a locked box. Mom gave it to me the day I graduated from the academy."* Trevor smiled at him, his white-blond hair cropped close in his preferred crew cut style and his blue eyes shining. *"I want you to have it."*

Randy jerked backward against the seat as if

he had received an electric shock. The watch had belonged to his former partner, Trevor Douglas. He had given it to Randy just two days before he was murdered. He had tried to refuse the gift, telling Trevor it belonged in his family and should be given to his son, Landon, instead. Trevor had insisted he take it, saying Randy was even closer to him than his own half brother, whom Trevor had only ever tolerated out of respect for his mom. According to Trevor, his half brother was his exact opposite and not someone he would ever have chosen as family or friend, given a choice.

After five years of working side by side putting criminals in jail, Randy also considered Trevor to be family. So, he had accepted the watch, thinking he'd return it later. Only later never came. Looking back, it was almost as if Trevor knew he was going to die.

Randy rubbed the back of his neck. Where was Katherine? He wanted to share his latest memory. He looked toward the entrance to the grocery store. What was taking her so long? A dark-color SUV like the one that had shown up at the cabin yesterday appeared in his peripheral vision. Slowly, he slid down in the seat and peeked out the back window, watching the vehicle as it turned into the parking lot, Torres at the wheel.

Opening the glove compartment, he pulled out the gun Sheriff Walker had given him and tucked it into his waistband. He slipped into the angler's vest, then shoved the file folder into the inside pocket. Placing the wide-brim hat onto his head, he casually exited the vehicle. A woman with two young children walked past him. He picked up his pace, trying to look like he was part of their group. Once he was in the store, he scanned the aisles, locating Katherine on the cereal aisle.

"What's wrong?"

"We need to get out of here. Torres just showed up." He took her arm and guided her toward the back of the store, leaving her shopping cart in the middle of the walkway. "I'm estimating there are sixty people in the store, counting customers and employees."

"What's your plan?"

"Not sure. Except to keep everyone inside this store safe. They shot a sheriff. I can't imagine they'd think twice about opening fire here," he said, not slowing his pace. "They would consider the murder of innocent people to be collateral damage if it meant killing us."

He paused behind an endcap and looked into the large convex security mirror mounted near the ceiling. Torres and two guys Randy didn't recognize entered the store. Torres stopped inside the front entrance, saying something to the men with him and motioning for them to search the store. The men quickly scurried in different directions, hunting them.

"It's obvious their arrival wasn't a coincidence," Katherine said, voicing his thoughts aloud.

"I was afraid of that. Okay, we can't slip out the front door with Torres standing guard. Time for plan B." Randy spotted double swinging metal doors near the meat section. "Come on."

They pushed through the doors and found themselves in a corridor. To their right was a door that led into a glass-walled room where the butcher worked—his back to them—cutting and packaging meat in full view of the customers. Katherine pointed to the large metal walk-in cooler to the left. "If they come this way, we can duck in there."

"That might work. Keep an eye on the butcher. Let me know if he spots us. I'll watch for Torres's friends." Randy peered out one of the small windows that was in the double doors.

One of the men walked past. His head turned in the direction of the aisles and away from the doors they hid behind. The other man walked up to him. "I don't see them anywhere. Do you?"

"No. But Torres says they're here, so we've gotta keep looking. Maybe they're hiding in the stockroom or the restroom or something. We'll have to check everywhere."

Randy stepped away from the window and opened the door to the cooler, motioning Katherine inside. Pulling the door closed behind them, he searched for something to slip under the door handle to secure it. Nothing.

"Hey, what are you guys doing in here?" Randy stiffened at the angry male voice that yelled from the other side of the door. Had Torres's men spotted them entering the cooler?

"Uh, we lost our friends and thought they might have come this way," one of the goons replied.

"Well, as you can see, they ain't in here. Now, get lost. You're blocking my cooler, and I've gotta get a slab of pork outta there."

Randy released a breath, the cold temperatures freezing it into a cloudy puff. They had to hide.

Ignoring the bitter-cold air that lashed at him, Randy grasped Katherine's arm and guided her to the back of the cooler, ducking behind large slabs of hanging beef. "Please, Lord, don't let them find us."

Katherine's teeth chattered. "I'm more worried about us turning into human Popsicles."

Without thinking through his actions, Randy wrapped his arms around her. She startled, but he pulled her closer. "Having each other's six means we look out for and protect each other's well-being, right? Wouldn't that include warding off frostbite? Now, hold still. We don't want the butcher to catch us."

He couldn't hear her mumbled response over the pounding of his heart. But she put her arms around his waist and stood really still. *You're simply offering aid to your partner. It's part of the job. No big deal.* Only, no matter what he tried to tell himself, he knew he was putting his heart in greater danger with every passing second.

ELEVEN

The cooler door opened, and Katherine held her breath. *Lord, please keep us safe.*

"I already told you to get outta here." The big burly butcher stood in the open doorway. "If you don't get movin', I'll forcibly remove you."

A tall, slender man in his late twenties with sun-bleached blond hair, who looked like he would belong at the beach with a surfboard if it weren't for his cowboy boots and the brown hat perched on his head, bobbed around behind the butcher and tried to look inside the cooler. Randy tightened his grip and pulled her farther into the shadow, cradling her to him with his back against the cold metal wall.

"Nick! Joe," Torres's voice boomed from the corridor. "Let's go."

"But boss, we ain't found them."

"Well, we're not going to find them here. I

don't know how they did it, but somehow, they slipped past us."

"Are you sure?"

"Of course I'm sure. I lost the…" Torres's voice faded as they walked away from the area.

"What do—" Randy placed his finger over her lips, halting her words as the butcher stepped inside the cooler. Curiosity about what Torres had lost had caused Katherine to forget the butcher's presence. She held her breath and waited.

"Annoying people. Who'd they think they'd find inside a cooler? No one in their right mind would hang out in here, unless they were part penguin or polar bear." The butcher came within three feet of their hiding place, muttering and grumbling under his breath as he selected a slab of pork. He lifted it and turned to leave, pausing at the door to glance once again into the cooler as if he were searching for them. Then he shook his head and started across the hall to his work area, the door of the cooler closing behind him.

The instant the latch clicked closed, Katherine released the breath she had been holding.

"That was close," Randy said, his warm breath brushing against her ear.

Suddenly, she found it difficult to breathe. Her heart raced, and the walls closed in on her.

She pushed free of Randy's arms and breathed in deeply. The cold air burned her throat, her chest constricting as she forced oxygen into her lungs.

"That's it. We're outta here." He clasped her hand and headed toward the door.

"But…what if…" She stopped in the middle of the cooler, swallowed and tried again. "They may still be out there."

He searched her face. "Why didn't you tell me you were claustrophobic? It could have been disastrous if you'd hyperventilated or passed out when those guys were here."

Claustrophobic? Where had he gotten that idea? "I'm not claustrophobic. I'm frozen." *And overwhelmed by emotions I haven't felt in a long time after being held in your strong arms.* Only she couldn't say that aloud.

"Then we really need to get you out of here so you can thaw." He smiled. "We'll go slow. Make sure the coast is clear before we go barreling into the open."

"Sounds like a plan."

He eased the door open and motioned for her to follow him into the corridor. The butcher was hard at work. The buzz of the electric slicer drowned out their footsteps as they moved to the double swinging doors leading into the shopping area. They peered through the windows. A woman with a toddler strapped into her shopping cart was examining the meat selections, and an elderly couple was picking out coffee creamer in the dairy section. No sign of Torres or his men.

"Okay, let's go." She casually strolled through the doors into the meat and dairy department, Randy following close behind. No one seemed to notice.

They paused beside the same endcap they had hidden behind earlier and scanned the convex security mirror once again. Could Torres and his men have really left just like that?

"If you'll keep watch, I'll make our purchases." She headed toward the shopping cart that still sat where she'd deserted it earlier.

Randy placed a hand on her arm, halting her. "Seriously? You want to take time to buy groceries?"

"It looks like Torres and his men have left the building. If they're waiting on us outside, the best thing we can do is blend in with the other shoppers. Leaving a grocery store without bags would look suspicious." Katherine paused and grinned, reaching out to touch the wide brim of the fishing hat he wore. "I like your disguise, by the way."

His face relaxed and the wrinkles on his

forehead softened. "You're probably right, but how are we going to disguise you?"

"I saw a rack of baseball caps and sunglasses when I entered the store. I'll pick up something there as I head to the checkout area."

"Okay, but if we see any sign of trouble, we're out of here, groceries or no groceries. Got it?"

Her heart smiled as she pushed the shopping cart toward the front of the store. Randy was being his old bossy self again. Only she was beginning to realize he didn't mean to come off as bossy. It was just his way of trying to control situations and not let things get out of hand. Why hadn't she realized that earlier? Giving orders came naturally to him, kind of like praying aloud. It was who he was. A take-charge kind of guy. It had taken him getting amnesia for her to see him in a different light.

What was it her mom used to say? *People who only look for the worst in others will never be disappointed because we are all flawed. Instead, always look at others with love and compassion so you can see the good inside them.*

Lost in thought, Katherine took a misstep and stumbled. Randy instantly caught her elbow and steadied her. Realization hit her like a lightning bolt. She was thawing out. And not just from the external cold she'd felt in the cooler, but the decade-old frozen tundra of her heart was also melting. She was falling for Randy.

That was it. She would have no choice but to request a transfer of post once they completed this assignment. Only, she vowed to herself, from this point onward, she would look at the world with open eyes and a renewed spirit, looking for the good in the world and not just the evil. *For ye were sometimes darkness, but now are ye light in the Lord: walk as children of light.* Ephesians 5:8. The long-forgotten scripture flitted through her mind.

Thank You, Lord, for not giving up on me and helping me remember I must be a light in this world. Lesson learned. Forgive me for my years of weakness. I won't turn from You again.

Randy scanned the parking lot as he waited for Katherine to finish making her purchases. There was no sign of Torres and his men or their SUV, but Randy doubted he would relax even the slightest bit until they reached the safe house.

Katherine walked toward him wearing a pink-and-brown camo baseball cap, her hair pulled through the back opening in a ponytail style. To complete her disguise, she wore an oversize pair of dark brown sunglasses that hid her eyes and part of her face, too. She carried several grocery bags. He reached for them. After a very slight hesitation, she relinquished the ones she held in her left hand. Randy took that as a good sign.

His memories hadn't fully returned. However, when she'd been talking about her brother, he had a brief memory of her being very independent and a little aloof, preferring to work alone whenever possible. He couldn't help but hope that the pattern they'd fallen into the past few days would be the norm from this point onward. They should always work together instead of independently.

They loaded up into the truck, and Katherine pulled out onto the highway. "The safe house is about seven minutes from here. Once we get out of this section of town, it will be backroads and open spaces."

"I'll watch for the SUV." Randy scanned the area as she drove. "You keep a lookout for a tail, in case they have more than one vehicle full of thugs looking for us."

She nodded as she checked the rearview mirror.

They rode in silence, no sign of anyone following them. Soon, Katherine turned into a subdivision of almost identical homes.

"We're here." She pulled to a stop in front of a nondescript brown brick house, put the truck into Neutral and activated the emergency brake. "Be right back."

Katherine hopped out, ran to the keypad, punched in a series of numbers and raced back to the truck as the garage door started upward. Pulling forward, she parked in the single-car garage. "I'll clear the house."

"Nothing doing." He pulled the sheriff's gun out of his waistband. "I'll clear the house. You check the perimeter. After we're sure the house isn't compromised, we'll close the garage door and take the groceries inside."

She looked as if she might argue with his orders, but thought better of it. Then she reached into her back pocket, retrieved a slender wallet, pulled a single key out from one of the credit card slips and handed it to him. They exited the vehicle, and she took off outside, her gun close to her body in a manner that wouldn't alert any of the neighbors.

There were two steps leading into the house. Randy stood to the side of them, unlocked the door and pushed it open. He listened. No sounds came from inside. His gun at the ready, he entered the house, stepping into a small kitchen with a dining nook. It was an older home with divided rooms and no straight sightlines. Slowly, working his way from room to room, he checked the approximately twelve-hundred-square-foot, three-bedroom, two-bath house. After he was convinced their hideout was secure and all doors and windows were locked, he headed to the garage.

Katherine stood beside the steps, waiting on him. He nodded, and she hit the button to lower the garage door. They slid their guns into their waistbands and collected the grocery bags, depositing them on the kitchen counter once they were inside.

"I hope we're not here long, but I bought enough supplies to last a week. Mostly sandwich stuff, cereal, soup, fruits and veggies. You know, stuff that doesn't require a lot of prep since neither of us likes to cook."

"That's good, but you know, if we're going to stay partners, one of us really needs to take a cooking class. Trevor was an excellent cook. Mostly Southern comfort foods, but he could also make some of the best enchiladas in the world." He started putting the milk, eggs, bacon and butter into the fridge. "After his dad died, his mom married a man who owned a ranch on the Texas-Mexico border. Trevor was sixteen and hadn't liked leaving all his friends and family in Mississippi. He didn't like horses or working outdoors, so he started helping the cook in the kitchen."

"Sounds like Trevor was an interesting person. I'm sorry I never got to meet him."

Randy straightened and turned to Katherine. "I think you would have liked him. We used to laugh at how an agent who detested horses and the outdoors got stuck working on this case." He sobered. Working on this case had cost Trevor his life. He'd left behind a wife and a thirteen-year-old son. "You know, I didn't want to accept the watch when he gave it to me. I felt like it belonged to his son, Landon, so after Trevor's funeral, I gave it to him. He was so happy to have it."

"That's right. You didn't start wearing the watch until recently." Katherine paused, a box of cereal midway to its place in the cabinet, and glanced over her shoulder. "How did you get it back?"

"Trevor's wife, Donna, returned it to me. She mailed it to the field office. I picked it up when I went to Denver last month." He fingered the watch crystal, noting it had stopped working again. Too bad Donna hadn't let Landon keep the watch. If she had, it wouldn't have gotten broken. "She included a note telling me I should keep it, since Trevor wanted me to have it. She said for me to use it as a reminder to not stop until I captured her husband's killers."

Katherine gathered the plastic grocery bags and tucked them into a drawer, then turned her attention to him. "That was nice."

"Yeah. Only, I still believe Landon should own the watch. After we put the León Dormido Cartel behind bars, I'll have it repaired and return it to him."

"Do you think his mom will let him keep it? I mean, she already returned the watch once."

"I think she'll let him accept it. Especially if I tell her we've put her husband's killers behind bars."

"Sounds like a good plan."

It would be. If it didn't take another two years to wrap up this case.

Randy's brow furrowed, and Katherine reached out her finger and touched the creases, wanting to smooth them and ease his turmoil. He captured her hand and pulled it to his chest. He leaned closer, his eyes searching hers. Was he going to kiss her? Did she want him to? Yes.

No. They were colleagues. They couldn't be anything more. She pulled away, breaking eye contact. "We have work to do. Find us something for lunch. I'll go retrieve the laptop, okay?"

Not waiting for his reply, she bolted from the room. What had gotten into her? She was an FBI agent with a job to do, not a high school girl with a crush on the star quarterback. She needed to remember that. Once the León Dormido Cartel was out of business, its leaders all behind bars, she would talk to Wanda about being reassigned to an office far away from Randy. Maybe there was an opening at the Anchorage office. She had always wanted to go to Alaska. It would be nice.

Keep kidding yourself. Maybe you'll even start believing it.

The instant Katherine stepped through the door to the bedroom she had used while Randy was missing, she immediately scanned the contents of the room. The red oak chest of drawers sat against the wall to the right of the door three inches off center, one drawer pushed in a little farther than the others. And the bed was perfectly made, except for a small corner of the patchwork quilt tucked under the mattress. Everything was exactly as she'd left it. She smiled. Growing up with a nosy little sister who loved hunting for Katherine's journal had taught Katherine to be creative when it came to catching people snooping through her things.

She knelt on the floor in front of the chest

of drawers. Pulling out the bottom drawer, she moved sweaters out of the way and accessed the hidden compartment. Her laptop, files and notes, along with her and Randy's Bureau-issued IDs and badges, were exactly where she'd left them. Gathering everything up, she headed back to the kitchen.

The smell of coffee and breakfast foods greeted her. Randy stood at the stove pouring beaten eggs into a hot skillet. "I hope you like omelets. It seemed like the easiest thing to cook."

Her stomach growled, and she laughed. "It smells delicious."

She carried the laptop and things over to the dining table, noting that the file Sheriff Walker had given them was already there.

"I grabbed that out of the truck."

"Do you think he's okay? He lost so much blood." The toaster popped, and she startled. "Sorry. I guess I'm a little tense."

Randy offered her a sympathetic smile as he started slathering butter on the hot toast. "It's okay. Why don't you call Richardson? Maybe she can check on the sheriff for us."

Katherine nodded and pulled the prepaid phone out of her back pocket. She punched in the number, and her finger hovered over the call button. Would Wanda answer a call from an unknown number?

"Let it ring twice. Then hang up. Wait fifteen seconds and call again. She'll answer," Randy said, as if he could read her mind.

"How—"

"Four years ago, I was working a case on the Canadian border when my phone ended up at the bottom of a lake. I bought a burner phone and called Richardson. She didn't answer until my third attempt." He shrugged. "So, we devised this method for future incidents."

"You remember a case you worked on four years ago, but you can't remember your ex-wife or the case you've dedicated two years of your life to solving?" She regretted the words as soon as they came out of her mouth. He couldn't help his amnesia. And his memories were returning. Not in one fell swoop like she would have hoped, but they were returning. "I'm sorry. I didn't—"

"It's okay." Randy offered a half smile and turned back to the stove. "Hurry and make the call before the food gets cold."

The food wasn't the only thing Katherine was afraid might run cold. With one thoughtless comment, she may have undone the feeling of camaraderie they'd shared the past few days. Then it would be back to following orders and not being a true partner.

TWELVE

Randy reached into the cabinet and retrieved two coffee mugs, filling each and carrying them to the table. Then he turned back to the stove to plate the food. All the while, trying not to eavesdrop as Katherine spoke to Wanda Richardson, which he found to be more of a challenge than he expected it to be. The desire to demand the phone and take over the conversation was surprisingly strong. Had he always been a person who gave orders and expected others to follow them? If so, it was a wonder Katherine had even bothered to look for him when he went missing. She had shown she was more than competent enough to handle any situation thrown at her. And other than her last question, she'd been nothing but considerate to him concerning his loss of memory. He suspected she hadn't meant the question to sound so harsh, but had instead spoken from a feeling of frustration.

To be fair, the entire situation frustrated him, too. He was also a bit apprehensive about the select memories his mind was still protecting him from. Because he believed his amnesia was shielding him from some piece of shocking information.

"Yes… Okay… I will." Katherine disconnected the call and placed the cell phone on the table. "Wanda said Sheriff Walker is out of surgery and is expected to make a full recovery."

"How does she know that already?" He handed her a plate with an omelet and a piece of buttered toast, then turned back to the stove to finish cooking his own meal.

"Yum." She tore off a piece of the bread and shoved it into her mouth. "This is so good."

"I should have made the phone call myself," he laughed. "Katherine, focus. How did Wanda know about the sheriff?"

"I knew it. Even with amnesia, you still have control issues," she said teasingly.

He gave her an exaggerated, shocked expression, and she rewarded him with sweet laughter.

"Okay. I won't keep you in suspense. The sheriff left instructions with his second-in-command to contact Wanda if anything happened to him. She got the first call at five this morning and has had hourly updates since."

Katherine added cream and sugar to her coffee and took a sip. "Mmm. I think you've been holding out on me the past year. I could have been eating omelets and drinking coffee instead of having a protein bar and Diet Coke each morning."

"That sounds totally unhealthy." He placed several napkins on the table and settled into the seat across from her. "Go ahead. Eat. We have a lot of work ahead of us if we plan to take down the cartel. So, we definitely need sustenance to keep up our strength."

"You don't have to tell me twice." She took a big bite of the omelet. "Seriously, you have to cook from now on."

The sheer joy she seemed to derive from a simple meal was evident by the smile on her face. There was limited time for cooking when working on a big case. Once they had the bad guys behind bars, he would have to fix her something better than an omelet. He could make her a juicy steak, or a roast with carrots and potatoes, or maybe grilled salmon. He'd let her choose. Unless… Randy froze. He swallowed, forcing the bite of food past the lump in his throat. She never had said if she was married or not.

Suddenly, a long-forgotten memory struck him, playing out in his mind's eye like one of the old home movies his mom always wanted to watch whenever he visited. He could clearly see the small one-story brick home he'd shared with his wife… Mandy…at Fort Bragg. The house had been basic military housing, a lot like the house he sat in now. The scene was eerily similar, too. Randy had cooked a meal for his wife. Only the mood was much different. Instead of appreciating his efforts, Mandy had criticized him for always making omelets or other breakfast-type foods. They'd gotten into an argument over the fact that she never seemed to do any housework or cooking, but she always complained he folded the towels wrong and never liked his meal choices.

He remembered their five-year marriage and how hard he had worked to make her happy. But he'd failed, miserably. Most likely because he had thought providing material things was showing love.

They had been high school sweethearts. After graduation, they had planned to attend college together, earn degrees and then marry. But Mandy was impatient. People said they were too young to marry, but they wouldn't listen. At age nineteen, Randy joined the military. He could get training in the field he wanted and could also continue his college degree while earning money to support a wife whose goal was to one day be a stay-at-home mom. It was the perfect setup, or so he thought.

When Randy talked to the army recruiters, they encouraged him to go the Special Forces route. At first Mandy wasn't excited about him being in Special Forces because the training process was much longer than infantry basic training, but once he pointed out the pay increase for being part of the elite forces, she was on board. She told him she'd miss him, but she could use the time he was away to plan the wedding of her dreams.

Things may have ended differently if only they had both spent as much time planning for their marriage as she had spent planning for the wedding.

"Randy... Randy!"

He jerked his attention to Katherine. "Oh, sorry. What?"

"You're doing it again. Spacing out." She tilted her head. "More memories?"

He nodded and shoveled another forkful of egg into his mouth. Maybe she'd take the hint that he didn't really want to discuss it. Not now anyway. These were his own private memories, not something that had to be shared to solve the case. He paused, feeling like a hypocrite. Hadn't he pushed Katherine to share personal details hours earlier? Yes, but in all fairness, his memories were still jumbled. *Yeah, right. Keep telling yourself that, buddy.*

Katherine watched the vein in Randy's neck twitch. It was obvious he was struggling with his most recent memory. Was he remembering his ex-wife? She wouldn't push him. If he wanted to share, he would. If not, well, she wouldn't say it was okay, especially since he'd been asking her a lot of personal questions, but she understood the need to keep certain things close. She didn't enjoy talking about her ex-fiancé, Nelson, either. Of course, who would like to admit their past mistakes and failed relationships? No one she knew.

Scooting back her chair, she stood and gathered their plates. "Why don't you look over the sheriff's files while I do the dishes."

"Let me help," Randy said as he pushed away from the table.

"Nothing doing." Katherine placed her hand on his shoulder and stopped him from standing. "You cooked. I'll clean. Now, get your notepad and pen and get to work."

"Yes, ma'am," he laughed, giving her a salute.

She shook her head, smiling as she crossed to the dishwasher.

A few minutes later, the kitchen cleanup

was complete. She refilled their coffee mugs and then settled into her seat opposite Randy, who was furiously scribbling notes. "Have you found anything interesting?"

"I'm not sure." He pushed the notepad toward her. "It seems the sheriff attended a state law enforcement conference a few months ago. One of the primary topics of the conference was illegal gambling and drugs. Chief Bradshaw and his wife, Dr. Grace Porter Bradshaw—"

"So, they got married!" Katherine had suspected there was a romance blooming when she saw them together last year.

Randy glanced up, his eyebrow cocked. "What?"

"Chief Bradshaw and Dr. Porter, the veterinarian he was protecting last year."

"Oh, yeah. Apparently. Anyway, the Bradshaws presented a seminar on the illegal horse racing that's been traveling around the state. They encouraged the officers present to be on the lookout for suspicious activity in all areas of the state." He used his pen to point to his notes as he continued. "Sheriff Walker has compiled a list of ranches in his area and listed notes about each of them. Nothing suspicious is jumping out about any of them, but

I've created a chart with the basic details on each one."

Katherine opened her laptop and powered it on. "A couple of those ranch names seem familiar, but that doesn't necessarily mean anything. A lot of horse trainers attend match races to scope out their competition for future legitimate races."

"But the match races are illegal, right? So, if we know the ranches participating, why haven't we arrested any of them yet?"

She continued to forget he still had large gaps in his memory. "Match races in and of themselves aren't illegal. Some would argue that it's nothing more than a practice match for the participants, much like a pickup game of basketball between members of opposing teams."

She finished typing in the password and hit Enter. Then she turned her attention back to Randy. "I'd hazard to guess most of the people gambling just see it as a friendly wager between neighbors. It never even crosses their mind that it's wrong. Likewise, they aren't aware of the drugs being sold to drug traffickers in the back of the stalls or the ones being pumped into the horses."

"I'm always surprised at how naive people can be."

Katherine shrugged. "I think people see what they want to see. Until they're faced with the harsh realities of this world, that is."

The way she had been when Jimmy died and Dad walked away from the family less than a year later. One would have thought being let down by the two men she loved most in the world as a child would have taught her that just because someone claimed to love you didn't mean they'd always do right by you. But it hadn't been until Nelson walked out on their wedding day that the reality that she couldn't depend on anyone but herself was really driven home.

"That's a very serious expression on your face. Are you okay?" Randy broke into her thoughts.

"Oh, yeah, I'm fine." She focused on the computer screen, selecting the appropriate file and opening it.

"I'm a good listener if you ever need to talk," Randy said.

She met his eyes, the concern etched in them deepening the blue to cobalt. After so many years of keeping things bottled inside, it surprised Katherine that she felt such a strong desire to share her burdens with him. But this wasn't the time. Besides, if she put it off, she was sure she'd get over this sudden need to share. "Thanks. I'll let you know if I ever decide to take you up on the offer. For now, we have work to do."

Randy scooted closer. She turned the screen so he could have a better view as she went over the files. "You may not remember, but Trevor took his laptop with him the day of his accident, and it was destroyed. However, every Bureau-issued laptop is set up to do an automatic cloud backup every evening. This means we still have access to his files. Unfortunately, his notes were scattered, and it's taken me months to get them into some form of organization."

"That doesn't make sense. Trevor was one of the most organized people I've ever worked with. He always used charts and graphs and was taking copious notes. Who do you think taught me to use a pen and notebook for organizing my thoughts?"

"Well, it didn't translate to his online file keeping. Maybe he was more old-school and technology just wasn't his thing."

"All I know is Trevor was one of the best agents around and I was blessed to have him as a partner and mentor."

Oh, how well she knew that. Randy had constantly praised Trevor's virtues, especially in the months following her error that led to Torres giving them the slip in Blackberry Falls.

Katherine would always come in second place in the partner department, and she was learning to be okay with that. After all, how could one compare to the memory of a beloved dead person?

Two hours later, papers lay strewn all over the table and a second pot of coffee brewed on the counter. Randy rubbed his eyes.

"Another headache? Do you need some meds?" Katherine scooted her chair back.

He placed his hand on hers, halting her. "No. Just a little eye strain from looking at the screen and all these notes." He sighed. "I feel like the information is right here, plain as day, but we're just not seeing it. You know? Like when my grandpa would look everywhere for his eyeglasses and they would be perched on top of his head."

"Yes, but when you keep looking and don't give up, you eventually find the things you're looking for… Oh, I forgot. I wanted to upload those photos into the NGI-IPS database to see if I can identify the man with Torres at the cabin yesterday."

Picking up her cell phone, she scrolled through the photos.

"May I see those?" Randy asked.

She handed the phone to him, and he studied

the image of the mystery boss man. Average height and a little chunky. Randy estimated the guy stood around five feet ten inches tall and weighed between two hundred and two hundred twenty pounds. He zoomed in to study the man's features. Brown wavy hair that grazed his collar. Chocolate brown eyes. And a mustache and beard trimmed close. Overall, the guy appeared ordinary. Not memorable. Someone who could easily blend into a crowd. Yet there was something about him that was very familiar. "I feel like I know this guy. His voice was the only one I recognized while we were hiding in the attic."

Katherine leaned close and shook her head. "Well, I've never seen him before. Perhaps he came to the stables one day while I wasn't there."

He handed her the phone. "Why don't you fill in some of my missing memories about the case. Maybe it will help me put the puzzle pieces together."

She connected the cell phone to the laptop via a small cable and started uploading the photos. Then she turned her attention to him. "I guess it can't hurt since most of your memories have returned."

Picking up his pen, he flipped to a blank page in the notebook. "I remember Trevor's death and working on the case up until that point. Also, thanks to what you've already told me, I remember bits and pieces of our time in Blackberry Falls. I don't remember how we tracked Torres to Wyoming or how we got jobs working at the stables."

"We spent months tracking down leads, hitting one dead end after the other. Then, one day you got out your notebook and started randomly doodling and jotting notes." Katherine smiled, a faraway look in her eyes. "It's common knowledge among your colleagues. When that notebook comes out, no one is to disturb you. I don't know what you'd call it. Brainstorming, maybe? That day you drew an image you'd seen on a matchbook Torres was using at the match race in Blackberry Falls. The image led us to a restaurant ten miles from here."

Randy looked at the page he'd been doodling on. He had drawn a moose head with the words *Moose Trail Restaurant* encircling it. Sliding the paper to Katherine, he asked, "Is this it?"

"Yes! Exactly." She glanced up, a look of amazement on her face. "Your mind never forgets a thing. It's just a matter of relaxing and letting the memories come to the surface on their own."

"I guess so." He tapped the pen on the table. "I remember being in the restaurant and overhearing Torres talking to Greg about needing to hire a stable hand to muck stalls and exercise the horses."

"That's right. You walked right up to Torres and told him you were new in town and needed a job. A couple of weeks later, you managed to get me a job as a housekeeper in Torres's home."

"Why did we go undercover as a married couple?"

"That was Wanda's idea. Dove Creek has a population of less than a thousand. If two strangers showed up in town at the same time, they needed to be connected some way to keep down suspicions. Wanda figured people wouldn't question us being together if they thought we were married."

A cold sensation snaked up Randy's spine, and he shuddered. Suddenly, his mind was transported back to the night of his accident. *He was in his vehicle, trailing Torres. Katherine had stayed at their rental house doing research. She wasn't aware he decided to trail Torres, hoping to find out who the boss man was calling the shots. Randy called her. Voice mail. Again. He gripped the steering wheel tighter. This was his fourth attempt to reach his partner. Most people he knew were practically glued to their phones, but not Agent*

Katherine Lewis. That woman never seemed to have her phone handy, or at least when they weren't together, and he needed to get in touch with her.

"That was why you spent so much time at the rental house doing research. You were trying to sort out Trevor's notes. I was angry when I couldn't reach you to tell you that I was tailing Torres." He pushed out of his chair and paced. "Why didn't you answer my calls? I was so worried about you. After my car went over the side of the mountain, I was hiding on a ledge. I overheard Torres say he gave the order for Greg to take care of you."

Katherine was suddenly beside him, her hands on either side of his face, forcing him to look at her. "It's okay. I got your message. And I was able to get to this safe house."

"I was afraid they'd killed you before you got my message." His voice cracked as emotion welled up inside him.

She dropped her hands and wrapped her arms around his body. "I'm sorry I worried you."

Her hug warmed him through to his core. He returned the embrace, burying his face in her hair. "Not answering your phone when working undercover is a very dangerous habit."

"I know. My phone was charging in the bedroom while I worked at the kitchen table. I didn't realize I had forgotten to turn the silent mode off after we returned from our stakeout at the stables the night before. It wasn't until I got up to stretch after being bent over a computer for hours that I went into the bedroom and saw the missed calls." Her voice softened with each word until it almost became a whisper. "I didn't mean to worry you."

Breaking the embrace, he lifted her chin and searched her face. The sorrow he saw etched in her eyes tightened his gut. Before his actions even registered with his brain, he tilted his head. His lips claimed hers as the strong urge to erase her pain engulfed him.

THIRTEEN

Katherine's head spun, her legs suddenly incapable of holding her upright. She clung to Randy for support. He deepened the kiss, leaving her even more breathless.

No. You shouldn't be doing this. He's your colleague just like Nelson was.

She placed her hands on his chest and pushed away, breaking the kiss but not the strong pull that wanted to draw her right back into his arms. She had to put some space between them.

"Excuse me." Katherine turned and headed down the hall. *Please, Lord, don't let him say anything.* She forced herself to walk at a normal pace and not run, even though she could feel his eyes boring into her retreating back.

She went into the bathroom, closed the door and leaned against it. Taking a few deep breaths, she willed her pulse to slow. Once she no longer felt like her heart was going to beat right out of her chest, she moved to the sink and splashed cold water on her face.

Katherine caught a glimpse of her reflection. Wide eyes looked back at her accusingly. "Don't judge me. I didn't initiate the kiss."

Didn't you? Weren't you the one who hugged him?

"It was a friendly gesture. Nothing more."

Yeah. Right.

"He looked vulnerable. I felt sorry for all he's been through."

You never hugged any of your former partners.

The truth hit her with the force of a tidal wave. She sank onto the edge of the tub and placed her head in her hands. "Dear Lord, I can't go through this again. It was humiliating to have my coworkers and family and friends witness Nelson walking out on me. Please let us find the evidence we need to put the cartel out of business. Then I'll move on to the next job."

In the ten years since her almost-wedding, she'd had very few dates. Working a job that consumed most of her waking hours meant there was very little time to find someone outside the Bureau. But that was okay. She didn't care if she never found love again, as long as she could continue to get drug dealers off the streets and behind bars. *Just keep reminding yourself of that.*

She stood, and after one last look in the mirror, she squared her shoulders and headed back into the kitchen.

Randy was at the table, looking over the notes. It was obvious he was unaffected by the kiss. She slowly released a breath. Okay. Act like nothing happened and everything will be fine.

"Did you find anything?"

He startled and looked up. "Are you o—"

"Did you find anything?" she questioned again, cutting him off. She didn't want to answer his questions about her reaction to the kiss. Not now. Solve the case first, then deal with extinguishing the spark that was building between them.

Meeting his gaze, she refused to blink or look away. He pressed his lips together, and his jaw twitched. For a moment, she thought he wouldn't let it go. Then he nodded and turned his attention back to his notes. She knew this wouldn't be the end of the discussion, but she was thankful for the small reprieve.

"Yes, actually. I think I may have found something important." He pulled a sheet of paper out of the file folder. "Sheriff Walker's list mentions the Edmond Oriol Stables just outside of Fort Collins, about ten miles from where I had my accident."

She sat in the chair she'd vacated earlier. "I'm not familiar with the place. It's never shown up on any of our reports as being connected to the match races."

"Possibly because they don't own any of the horses. They're a training facility, but they only work with the animals from age eighteen to twenty-four months. After that point, the horses move to different training facilities." He tapped his pen on the notepad. "Several of the horses that have gone through their stables have won elite racing titles. But because the horses were training at a different facility once they began racing, Edmond Oriol Stables remained in the background. At least as far as the public was concerned. Why do you suppose they'd want to give up the prestige and recognition?"

"That is curious. What else did you discover?"

"According to the sheriff's files, the owner of Edmond Oriol Stables is Victor Reyes."

She frowned and shook her head. "Is he someone I should know?"

"No. But I know him." Randy looked up at her, a troubled expression on his face. "He's Trevor's half brother."

Katherine gasped. "You think Trevor's half brother is mixed up in this? Could he be responsible for Trevor's murder?"

"I think it's possible."

"Doesn't that seem a bit farfetched? There has to be more than one man in this world named Victor Reyes."

"Could be, but I don't believe in coincidences. Especially since Edmond Oriol is an anagram for León Dormido."

Randy wanted to be wrong, but deep inside his gut, he knew he'd discovered an important piece of the puzzle. The thought that Trevor could have been murdered by his younger brother was sickening. Randy would not stop until he uncovered the truth. If he was right and Victor had even the smallest role in Trevor's murder, Randy would see that he was arrested and put in jail for a long time. Not only for Trevor but also for Landon and Donna. Randy would do all he could to keep Trevor's wife and son safe. He owed that to his former partner.

For the next four hours, Randy and Katherine worked side by side, slowly untangling the web that connected Victor to the match races. All in all, the Edmond Oriol Stables had trained over two-thirds of the horses that the

FBI knew had participated in the match races in Colorado.

"There has to be a connection between the Edmond Oriol Stables and the Triple R Ranch." Katherine scrolled through the document she had pulled up on the laptop.

"Triple R Ranch?"

She sighed. "I forgot. You still have a few blank spots in your memory. Triple R is the name of the ranch where we've worked undercover for the past two months."

"Oh, right. Who owns Triple R Ranch?"

"Antonio Torres is listed as the owner on the property records. He bought it six years ago but only started living there and actually turning it back into a working ranch after he gave us the slip last year."

"Who owned it before him?"

She clicked a few keys and pulled up a different website. "Xavier Reyes." Her eyes widened. "Is he related to Victor?"

Randy took in a deep breath, releasing it slowly as he tried to calm his mind. "That's the name of Victor's father. Trevor's stepfather. If I remember the story correctly, Trevor's dad passed away when Trevor was ten years old. For the next five years, it was just him and his mom. She worked as a waitress to support them. The summer Trevor turned fifteen, Xavier Reyes—a smooth-talking well-to-do man—came through town. He and Trevor's mom had a whirlwind romance, marrying just three months later. Victor was born a year later. Two years after that, Trevor enlisted in the air force. The day after he graduated high school."

"So, I take it Trevor never got along with Xavier?"

"Didn't seem like it. Of course, he never really talked about his ex-stepfather a whole lot. Everything I just shared was pieced together from random bits dropped in conversations here and there."

"Do you think Trevor knew his stepfather and half brother were involved with the León Dormido Cartel?"

"No. He would have told me if he knew something like that. It would have been important for the case." The last week of Trevor's life played out in Randy's mind. The gift of the wristwatch. Their last morning together, drinking coffee and going over the plans for the day. Trevor's insistence that if anything happened to him, Randy was to make sure Donna followed the instructions he'd left in their safe-deposit box. He wanted his wife and son to relocate to a small town so Landon could have a better life. "Actually, now that

I think about it, I wonder if Trevor stumbled upon the truth just before he was murdered. But why wouldn't he have told me?"

"I don't know. Is his mom still living? If so, maybe he wanted to be sure to have all the facts before accusing his stepdad and brother."

"Yes. I met her at Trevor's funeral." Randy pictured his former partner's mother, a petite gray-haired woman who had clung to her only surviving child. "Victor was with her, but I didn't exchange more than a few words with him. Xavier wasn't there, though. He and Trevor's mom divorced after Victor graduated high school. Trevor said she took her divorce settlement and moved to Florida."

Randy got up to pour himself another cup of coffee, his fourth for the day. He snagged the vanilla creamer out of the fridge and added a generous amount to his cup. Then he filled the mug with the rich, dark coffee, steam wafting up and filling his nostrils with the sweet scent. He took a sip and turned back toward the table, stopping midway as another lost memory invaded his thoughts.

He was in a small conference room. There was a divorce mediator sitting at the head of the table. A stern-looking woman, she reminded him of his seventh-grade English teacher. A no-nonsense person who expected things to go a certain way and for all parties involved to follow the rules. Randy sat on one side of the table with his lawyer beside him. Mandy was across from him with her lawyer on one side of her and Major Chad Billings, his former squadron leader, on the other. Randy could not believe that Mandy had brought the man she'd left him for to their divorce mediation. Major Billings was seventeen years Mandy's senior and had retired from military life to avoid prosecution when the affair came to light.

"Are you okay?" Katherine stood beside him, the all-too-common look of concern on her face.

"Yes. I just never know when a random memory is going to strike." Randy slid back into his seat. "Now, let's see what other connections we can uncover between Torres and Xavier Reyes. I have a feeling there's more to it than the simple fact that Torres purchased property from Reyes."

Katherine hesitated, as if she were waiting for him to share his memory. When he didn't, she settled back behind the laptop and pulled up a web search engine. Randy hated that his memory gaps caused her concern, but some things were too private to share. No one needed to know his failure to make his wife happy had resulted in her having an affair, causing their divorce. Looking back, he realized he had spent most of their married life trying to placate Mandy. Starting on their honeymoon when he had used his emergency credit card to book a weekend stay at a luxury resort after she hated the camping trip he had planned because of their limited budget, and ending with him leaving the military in an attempt to save their marriage—thinking the long deployments were what had caused the breakdown of their union. Only his decision to leave the military had happened too late since Mandy and Major Billings had already begun their affair.

He wondered if Mandy and her major were still together, and if she was happy now. What had his mom always told him when he was growing up? True happiness comes from within and should never depend on the actions of others.

Katherine was an independent woman who didn't need others to make her feel a sense of self-worth. How he'd ever confused her with Mandy when he'd first woken in the hospital was beyond his comprehension. Other than their hair color, they were nothing alike.

He regretted not discussing the kiss earlier, but the look in Katherine's eyes had told him any such discussion wouldn't be welcomed or end well. Randy was sorry the kiss had upset her, but he wasn't sorry he'd followed through with the impulse.

Would he have had a successful marriage if he'd waited to marry someone like Katherine? No, not someone like her. No denying it. Randy wished he and Katherine hadn't simply been undercover agents pretending to be married. He wanted to be her husband. Two things made it impossible for him to ever pursue that reality: his lack of knowledge about her personal life and the fact that he never wanted to be in the position to fail her the way he had Mandy.

FOURTEEN

Katherine bolted upright in bed. What day was it? She pulled her phone off the bedside table. Sunday. 2:37 a.m. She had almost forgotten. The next match race was tomorrow afternoon. It was scheduled to take place somewhere in Colorado for the first time in nearly a year. The name of the venue escaped her.

She kicked free of the covers tangled around her feet and made her way across the room to the light switch. The Bureau really needed to invest in some bedside lamps for their safe houses. Making her way back to the bed, she sat down and reached for her wallet. For convenience, she carried a small billfold similar to what many of her male counterparts carried. Much easier to put into a pocket and less cumbersome than a purse.

Pulling out the folded slip of paper she kept tucked into one of the card slots, she smiled at the realization that Randy's note-taking habit had rubbed off on her. Sometime early in their partnership, she'd gotten into the habit of keeping paper handy for any necessary notes.

In the excitement of the last few days, searching for Randy and then discovering he had amnesia, she had forgotten she'd jotted down important race information the day he disappeared. It had been her morning to clean Torres's house. Normally, Edna, the full-time housekeeper who had worked and lived on the property since Torres first purchased it, was the only one allowed in Torres's suite. But she had twisted her ankle and couldn't climb the stairs.

Katherine had convinced Edna to let her clean the upstairs rooms, giving her an opportunity to snoop. She'd found a small datebook in one of the nightstands. A fount of information had been held within its pages, with notes on all the match races—past and future—including dates, locations and times. Snapping pictures with her cell phone would have been her preference, because she could have gotten all the information.

But Torres had a guard who monitored the goings and comings of all people entering his residence. Part of the guard's daily responsibilities was to confiscate employees' cell phones, locking them in a safe until the end of their shift. According to Edna, Torres didn't want his employees distracted by phone calls or text messages while they were on the clock. Katherine suspected he was just as afraid of someone taking selfies and capturing things in the background that he didn't want posted on social media and subsequently leaked to the authorities.

Katherine had quickly jotted down all the info she could, including details about the three races scheduled for this month. One of the guards had come in mere seconds after she'd closed the drawer with the datebook safely back in its place, demanding what was taking so long. She pretended she had just finished dusting, gathered her supplies and left.

She had meant to discuss her discovery with Randy when he drove her back to the rental at lunchtime, but Greg had sent him to Cheyenne to pick up some supplies. She'd ended up hitching a ride with Edna, who was headed to a doctor's appointment. Once back at the rental, Katherine had started working on deciphering Trevor's research, forgetting about her own notes.

Unfolding the paper, she went straight to the information about tomorrow's match race. The race was scheduled to begin at 3:00 p.m. at a ranch that bordered the state line.

When she had jotted down the notes, she'd been focused on getting the words written quickly and hadn't really focused on what she wrote. Looking over the rest of the notes and truly reading the words for the first time, she gasped. *Edmond Oriol Stables. Meeting with Xavier and sons @ 2:00 p.m. Festivities begin @ 4:00 p.m. April 24*. Today! Her heart raced. All the key players behind the León Dormido Cartel were going to be in one place. This was their chance to arrest them. Would they be able to obtain a search warrant in time? She needed to call Wanda. The prepaid phone was still on the kitchen table.

Changing into jeans and a sweatshirt, she crossed to the door, clicked off the light and padded down the hall. Randy needed his rest. She'd let him sleep as long as she could.

There was a faint light coming from the kitchen, and she heard someone moving around. Had Torres's men found them? Backtracking to the bedroom, she retrieved her gun from the nightstand.

Pausing outside Randy's door, she debated waking him but decided against it. She'd investigate the noise first.

Staying close to the wall, she worked her way through the living room and peered around the doorway into the kitchen. Randy sat at the table, drinking a glass of milk as he looked over the files spread out on the table, the light from the range hood casting an eerie glow.

"You know, creeping around in the middle of the night is a surefire way to get yourself killed," she said, laying her gun on the table.

Randy smiled. "I heard you moving around in your room. I figured you were having as much trouble sleeping as I was. So, I thought I'd get a head start looking over the rest of the files and wait for you to join me."

Laughter bubbled up inside her, and she didn't even try to tamp it down. This was the Agent Randy Ingalls she knew and loved. Loved? She pressed her lips together. No. *Knew and loved* was just an expression, not a self-declaration of feelings.

Randy set down his glass and pushed away from the table. He flipped on the light switch, blinking in the brightness that bathed the room. "I didn't mean to alarm you."

"It's okay." She slid into a chair and powered up the laptop. "But next time, when you hear me moving around, knock on my door to let me know you're awake."

Katherine was all business, and it saddened him. Even though it had been short-lived, he'd liked the sound of her laughter. He wished he knew what thoughts had flitted through her beautiful head to make her clam up so suddenly.

"What woke you?" they asked in unison and then smiled.

The tension that had entered the room moments ago was broken. *Thank You, Lord.*

"I managed to sleep a couple of hours, but I had trouble turning my brain off." He offered her a smile. "I'm pretty sure I've remembered everything now."

"Everything? Even your wife?"

"Ex-wife. And yes. The marriage ended almost two decades ago, and there are no lingering feelings, on either side."

"I'm sorry."

"Don't be. Now, what woke you?"

"Oh, yeah." Katherine jumped up and darted out of the room, the sound of her footsteps fading as she went down the hall. She returned as quickly as she'd left and handed him a piece of creased paper. "I didn't get a chance to tell you before you disappeared, but I was able to get into Torres's private chambers. I found a datebook and jotted down as much information as I could."

She leaned over him, her hair brushing against his face. He instinctively reached up and pushed it behind her ear. Katherine recoiled. A pang of sadness gripped him.

"Oh, sorry." She slipped the ever-present hair tie off her wrist and put her hair into a ponytail. Leaning back down, she pointed to the paper. "The next match race is tomorrow, but look at this. Xavier and his sons are meeting with Torres today. Do you know what that means?" Excitement punctuated her words.

"Hang on. Give me a chance to look it over." He read the paper. "So, Xavier is coming to Colorado. When I talked to Wanda earlier, she said the last known address for him was in Cancún, Mexico."

"You talked to Wanda?"

"After you went to bed and I was sure all of my memories had returned, I used the prepaid phone to let her know all was well. I also wanted to check on Sheriff Walker. She said he's recovering. He should be released from the hospital this morning, but he'll be on medical leave for at least a month." Randy pictured the lawman who'd helped them escape Torres's men and provided them with shelter. "I doubt he'll be thrilled to take forced time off, especially if it involves physical therapy to regain strength in his injured shoulder."

Katherine smiled. "I imagine you're right."

"Did you know he's the one who found me after my accident?"

"No, I didn't. That explains the extra interest he seemed to have in your case and why he grilled me at the hospital." She settled back into her seat. "Did you and Wanda discuss the case?"

"I asked her about Xavier and Victor. She said Xavier has been on the Bureau's radar for years, but they've never had anything concrete they could arrest him for."

"Well, this is our chance. All we have to do is connect him to the match races and the León Dormido Cartel." Fire sparkled in her eyes. "We need to call Wanda right now and get her working on a warrant so we can finally bring Xavier Reyes to justice for his crimes, including the murder of a federal agent."

Even though he knew getting a search warrant on such short notice was going to be tough, her excitement and the thought of finally getting justice for Trevor's murder had him reaching for the phone.

Randy put the phone on speaker so Katherine could be part of the conversation.

"If this isn't an urgent matter, I'm going have you relocated to the most miserable location I can find for the rest of your tenure with the Bureau."

Randy quickly filled his boss in on their discovery. Wanda's annoyance at being woken at such an early hour dissipated quickly once she learned of the intended meeting.

"So, you see, we have less than ten hours to get a warrant and put a plan in place to arrest these guys." Katherine's excitement had waned a bit as they spoke to the SAC.

"I guess it's a good thing I started the paperwork to initiate a search warrant after I got off the phone with Randy earlier." The sounds of Wanda moving around and drawers being opened and closed echoed in the background. Their boss was fully awake and in take-charge mode. "I was just waiting for the right info to complete it. I'll head into the office now and get the ball rolling. In the meantime, you two figure out how you're going to get on the Edmond Oriol Stables property undetected. I'll need you to keep close tabs on Xavier and Victor. Wait a minute. Didn't you say the meeting was with Xavier and sons?"

"That's what Torres had written in the datebook," Katherine answered.

"The Bureau doesn't have a record of Xavier having more than one son. Randy, did Trevor ever mention stepbrothers?"

"No. He only spoke about his half brother."

"Could Xavier have had other children after

his divorce from Trevor's mom?" Katherine asked.

"I guess that's possible, but the child would be really young. Would he bring a teenager to one of these meetings?" Randy didn't like the thought of someone so young being dragged into the family business of drugs and gambling.

"It's not unheard of in cartels. They like to train the children to take over the business, much like being born into a royal family. You have no say in your future career. Everything is planned out for you. I'll see what I can find out on the identity of this unknown son. If he was born in Mexico, it may be harder to get info on him." Wanda sighed.

"Wanda, before you go, are there any updates on the mole in the agency?" Katherine asked.

"No. Nothing. So, that means, besides you two and myself, no one else is to know what's going down today until the last minute. Got it?"

"Yes, ma'am," Randy and Katherine said in unison.

"After I get the warrant, I'll head your way with backup."

They disconnected the call. Adrenaline

surged through every fiber of Randy's being. *This is it, Trevor. The day we get justice for your murder.*

FIFTEEN

Katherine lifted the binoculars to her eyes and scanned the Edmond Oriol Stables property. Heavily armed guards were stationed at the entrance. If the large white tents and catering trucks were any indication, Victor was preparing for a big celebration of some sort.

"Whatever the festivities are, I'd say they're expecting several hundred people by the number of tables and chairs I saw unloaded." She turned to Randy, who was seated next to her looking through his own pair of binoculars. They were parked on a dirt road behind a row of trees that bordered the property, about two miles south of the activity.

"If we can find a way past the guards, a crowd could work in our favor, helping us blend in." Randy was ever the optimist.

"I'm pretty sure this is an invitation-only event where your name has to be on a list or something. Driving up claiming to be a guest won't work."

"No, but what if we're part of the catering staff?" Randy lowered his binoculars. "My aunt owned a catering company. When I was a teenager, I'd work weekends and summers as a server anytime she needed extra help. For an event this large, she would hire temps. We never met most of them until the day of the event."

"Sounds like a good plan. Only, how do we get hired on such short notice?"

"Leave it to me." He picked up the phone. "Read me the number off the side of the catering truck."

She did as instructed and then waited quietly while Randy made the phone call. Soon, he had convinced the person he was speaking with that they were husband and wife, new to the area, and the temp agency had told them about the job. They were so sorry to be calling so late on the day of the event, but they really could use the work. And yes, they had experience.

"Yes. I understand. Thank you." Randy disconnected the call. "I spoke with Margaret, the owner of the catering company. She said all the waitstaff positions have been filled, but she could use one more sous-chef. She said if you can get to the restaurant in twenty-five minutes, the job is yours."

"But what about you? How are you getting onto the property?"

"Drive. I'll fill you in on the ride."

She started the truck and backed out of their hiding spot. At the end of the dirt road, she turned right, headed toward Fort Collins and away from Victor Reyes's property.

Randy entered the address into the maps app on the phone. "Didn't you say you rented a car to get to the hospital where I was transported after the accident?"

"That's right. A small compact car. Why?"

"The restaurant is three blocks from the hospital. I thought we'd swing by there and pick up the rental car. Wanda can notify Sheriff Walker where to find his friend's truck. Then, after you get your uniform, name tag and letter stating that you're part of the staff, we'll head back to Victor's ranch."

"Okay, but that still doesn't tell me how we get you onto the property."

"The box trucks, catering vans and staff were going through the side entrance. While there were two guards at the front entrance, there was only one at the side one." Randy smiled. "For whatever reason, that guard didn't deem it necessary to look inside the rear of the vehicles or the trunks."

It took a moment for his words to sink in. She was going to be the one undercover, and Randy was going to be the one in the trunk. Before his accident, he never would have allowed her to be the one in the driver's seat, literally and figuratively. Did this mean he truly trusted her now and forgave her for letting Torres escape the last time?

"You're being awfully quiet. Do you have a better plan?"

"No. I was just going over the details in my head. I think you're right. It's our best option." There was no way she was going to question him or plant the idea into his head that he should be the one who drove them through the gates and dealt with the guards. She needed to prove herself to him, let him see that one mistake didn't define her as an agent.

Katherine pulled into the parking garage at the hospital and located the rental car. The only available space was five spots away, so she pulled into it and parked. "What are we going to do about the keys? We can't really lock them in the truck without knowing if the sheriff has a spare."

Randy shrugged. "I'll hide them in the front

bumper. Should be fine until Sheriff Walker can send someone to get the truck."

They swapped vehicles and Katherine quickly drove them to the restaurant, located in what appeared to be the downtown area, with quaint shops and boutiques. She parked on a side street and prepared to exit the vehicle.

"Hang on." Randy placed a hand on her arm. "Do you have any money or a credit card? I can't go into the party dressed like this." He swept his hand down his torso, indicating the green plaid shirt and dark blue jeans he'd changed into this morning.

"Hmm. I guess you're right." She looked around and saw a men's clothing store across the street. Digging into her back pocket, she retrieved her wallet and handed him a few of the large bills she kept on hand in case of emergency. "Here you go."

"Thanks. I'll make sure the Bureau pays you back. See ya in fifteen minutes or less." He exited the car and dashed across the street. A man on a mission.

Dear Lord, please, let this work. I get nervous when a plan is thrown together like this and not mapped out clearly. But I know, with You guiding us, the way will be lit. Her heart settled into a normal rhythm, and her nerves eased. How had she not realized what comfort there was in casting your cares on the Lord?

She opened her door. It was time to put this plan into motion.

Exactly fifteen minutes later, Randy exited the clothing store. He had swapped his plaid shirt for a crisp white button-down, open at the collar, and a dark blazer. He'd also changed his brown work boots for a pair of black cowboy boots. To complete the look, he'd added a black cattleman-style cowboy hat.

Katherine wasn't back at the car, yet. She was probably filling out paperwork or something. He leaned against the hood and watched the people milling about. A family—mom, dad and three kids whom he guessed ranged in age from one to six—were enjoying ice cream at an outside table at a nearby ice cream shop. The kids were enjoying the treat. Especially the little girl with her hair in pigtails who had chocolate smeared all over her pink dress. Her father laughed as he tried to wipe a layer of the sticky treat off her hands and face.

A pain stabbed Randy's heart. He had wanted kids. If he and Mandy had stayed married, he very well could have had a couple who would have been high school or college age by now. At forty-two, he wasn't too far from the age of some grandfathers. Had he missed his chance to have children, and grandchildren, of his own one day? Why had he allowed his anger at Mandy to eat at him all these years and prevent him from finding love again?

"Well, what do you think?" Katherine walked toward him dressed in black slacks and a white button-down, her hair pulled back into a single braid that hung over one shoulder.

His heart skipped a beat. The love he had waited his whole life for had been right in front of him for the past year. *Lord, please keep her safe today. I really need the opportunity to tell her how I feel once this case is wrapped up.*

"You look great. Like a sous-chef."

"And you, sir, clean up very nicely. You look like one of the horse owners that frequent Torres's ranch." Her fingers caressed the brim of his cowboy hat. "Nice touch. You can use it to help shield your face."

"That's what I'm hoping." He opened her car door, something he'd never done for her or any other partner before. She gave him a strange look, a light pink hue coloring her face, but slid into her seat wordlessly.

They rode in silence back to the wooded area where they'd hidden earlier watching the goings and comings at the Edmond Oriol Stables. Once parked, Katherine pulled out the prepaid phone. "Still no word from Wanda. Should I call her?"

"No. She said she'd text us with updates. I'm sure she's busy getting the warrant and putting a team together to storm the place." He lifted the binoculars to his eyes. "We'll go through with our plan to access the property and keep a watch on the Reyes family and make sure they don't give us the slip before backup arrives."

Katherine pulled a phone out of her back pocket and handed it to him. "This is my FBI-issued cell phone. I've reset the passcode to to-day's date. It's probably best to keep it off for now since we've not been able to identify the mole. But, if we get separated, I wanted you to have it in an emergency."

"Thanks." He tucked it into his blazer.

"Okay, let's do this." She pushed the release to open the trunk and they exited the car. "Are you sure you're going to fit in that small space?"

He peered in at two overflowing laundry bags that filled the trunk. "Laundry?"

"I had to get our belongings out of the rental house somehow. The only thing I could think was to pile everything into laundry bags and tell the kid who drove me to town that our washing machine had gone out." She shrugged. "I left everything in the trunk and only carried a few things into the safe house. If I would have known we'd have to ditch the rental car, I would have lugged it all inside."

"It's okay." He tried to give her a reassuring smile. Randy hated to see her so defensive. He'd obviously done a number on her self-esteem when he'd gotten angry at her for leaving her post in Blackberry Falls. "You did great. That was quick thinking. And it all worked out. Especially since the last agents who used the safe house left clothes behind that fit me."

He pointed to the blue-and-white license plate frame proclaiming the name of the rental car company. "I need to remove that. I doubt there's a screwdriver in the glove compartment. Would you happen to have a coin or something?"

She disappeared into the car. When she returned, Katherine held her hand out triumphantly and displayed a couple of dimes, three pennies and a quarter. "I stopped at a fast-food restaurant for coffee and a Danish the morning I found you. Fortunately, I dropped the change into one of the cup holders."

"Perfect." He took a penny and knelt behind the vehicle. Soon the rental car logo was no longer on display.

Randy lifted the oversize canvas bags out

of the trunk, tucked the license plate frame under the mat and climbed inside. "Actually, the clothes may be a good thing. They can be used to hide me. Open one of the bags and dump it on top of me. I don't think the guards will want to dig around in a pile of laundry."

"Won't they wonder why I have a bunch of clothes in the trunk?"

"I'm sure you'll come up with a good excuse." He winked and lay down, curling his knees up in front of his body and tucking the new cowboy hat behind him. *Tick. Tick. Tick.* He looked at the watch on his wrist. The seconds hand was moving. Randy smiled as a sense of peace settled over him. The watch working again was almost like Trevor being there encouraging him and letting him know everything was going to be okay.

Katherine dumped the clothes out of one of the laundry bags, covering Randy in a blanket of jeans and plaid work shirts. If she focused, she could make out the outline of his body. Hopefully, it was simply because she knew he was there and anyone else looking into the trunk would only see clothes. Finally, she pulled out a third of the clothes from the second bag and scattered them around before she hoisted the bag and tossed it on top of the pile.

"Umph."

"Sorry."

"It's okay." He laughed. "I exaggerated a bit. Tell me, how's everything look? Do you think we'll pull it off?"

She sighed. "I hope so, but you may want to send up a prayer."

"I already have."

Katherine closed the trunk and slid back into the driver's seat of the rental, sending up a silent prayer of her own.

In a matter of minutes, she was at the gate, fourth in line behind two box trucks and a van awaiting admittance. There were two guards on duty now. One with a clipboard who spoke to the drivers. One with an assault rifle who walked around the vehicles, peering into windows and opening the back doors and hatches to check the contents.

She ran through an imagined scenario in her head, how she'd answer the guards' questions and what to do if the one with the weapon insisted on looking inside the trunk. Soon, it was her turn.

"What's your business?" the bored-looking guard asked, glancing at the paper on the clipboard.

"I'm with the catering service."

This got his attention. He jerked his head upward, looking at her for the first time.

"I'm a sous-chef," she said, trying to remain casual as the other guard walked around her vehicle.

"The catering crew has been here for nearly two hours. Why are you just now arriving?"

"I don't know about that. I just left the restaurant and was told to come straight here." Katherine handed him the letter from the catering company owner stating that she was part of the staff for the event.

He read over the letter. "Mr. Reyes isn't going to be happy. All of the catering staff were supposed to arrive together in no more than two vehicles. He doesn't want extra vehicles cluttering up the space."

It sounded like Victor Reyes and Antonio Torres both had control issues. She tamped down the response she wanted to give and smiled at the guard. "All I know is the chef preparing for this big shindig is working understaffed. If you want to be responsible for things not being prepared on time, I'll turn around and go tell my boss I wasn't allowed in."

"Reyes Senior won't like his meal being messed up." The other guard had come to stand beside her door. "I say we let her in, but first," he said, turning to her, "I need you to pop the trunk so I can see inside."

"I can't. The release latch is broken."

"Then open it with the key." He bent down to glare at her. "Or I'll take an ax to it. Either way, I'm looking inside before you go through those gates."

She put the vehicle into Park and turned off the engine. Climbing out, she headed to the back of the car, complaining all the while. "Such a waste of time. All you're going to find inside are clothes."

"It's my time to waste. Now open it." He gestured to the trunk with the butt of his rifle.

She did as he instructed while calculating the self-defense moves she would need to use to overpower him and take his gun if he spotted Randy. With a click, the trunk released and the bored clipboard guard pushed it upward.

"What? It really is full of clothes," assault rifle guard said in astonishment.

"I told you."

"Yeah, but what's this?" He reached in and pulled out a man's undershirt. "These are men's clothes." He bent farther inside and then straightened, the black hat Randy had worn earlier in his hand. "What else are you hiding under here?"

"Ugh," she huffed, yanking the shirt and hat out of his hands and tossing them back into the trunk. "These are my boyfriend's clothes. Ex-boyfriend, I mean. After catching him with Belinda Sue, I decided I'd had enough of his cheating ways. I also figured a low-down no-good cheater didn't deserve to have anything more than the clothes on his back, so when I cleared out of our apartment, I took all his clothes, too."

The larger guard used the barrel end of his rifle and poked down through the clothes, pulling it back out with one of her lace-trimmed undershirts dangling from the end.

"That's enough." Snatching the item of clothing off the assault rifle and dropping it back onto the pile, she slammed the trunk and faced the guard. "I'd just as soon do without a day's pay than to stand here while you rummage around through my undergarments."

The smaller guard made a hasty retreat, moving on to the next vehicle in line, obviously not wanting to deal with an irate female. Katherine bit the inside of her lip to stop the smile that threatened, praying the weapon-toting guard's fear of upsetting his bosses with a delayed meal outweighed his fear of allowing her entrance.

"Alrighty. You're cleared to enter. Follow the drive around to the left side of the house. You'll see where the other service provider vehicles are parked. The stone-paved walkway will lead you to the kitchen door."

"Thank you. And I'm sorry. Thinking about my ex riles me up."

"Just go." He waved her on.

Pulling through the gate, Katherine smiled at the look on the guard's face. Pride swelled through her. She was becoming a great actress. The thought sobered her. Proverbs 16:18 came to mind. *Pride goeth before destruction, and an haughty spirit before a fall.*

"I hear You, Lord. The last few days I have finally learned I am nothing without You," she whispered as she drove through the double black iron gates.

This mission had only succeeded to this point with the Lord's help. And with Randy's. What was it the preacher had said to her and Nelson when they attended their pre-wedding marriage counseling? A cord of three was stronger than a single strand. Relying on the Lord to be the most important strand in a partnership guaranteed a strong, unbreakable bond that could overcome all obstacles.

The Lord. Her. And Randy. Katherine's

breath caught. Was Randy the partner she needed all along? Could he possibly feel the same about her? Only one way to find out, but that required getting through the mission today alive.

SIXTEEN

Randy smoothed his wrinkled clothing the best he could with his hands and placed the cowboy hat on top of his head. "That was close. I thought the guard was going to reach in and grab me. But you did a great job throwing him off."

"Thanks," Katherine replied distractedly as she surveyed the area.

A large white delivery truck pulled up beside them. Two men jumped out and started hastily unloading tablecloths and crates of what he could only assume was dishware. A florist's van was parked next to the house and oversize centerpieces of yellow roses and white orchids were being unloaded and carried toward the large white tent in the backyard.

Katherine leaned in and whispered, "I don't know what the celebration is, but Victor isn't sparing any expense."

"Seems like. Okay, you go into the kitchen

and find the chef. See what you can discover about the party and the reason for the celebration. I'll look around and see if I can find where Victor and Xavier are holding their meeting."

"I don't like separating, especially since we don't have our earbuds or anything to help us communicate."

"I know, but we don't have much choice. With you in a catering uniform and me dressed like a guest, we'd draw too much attention walking around together."

Two muscular men dressed in black suits rounded the corner of the house, their jackets flapping open and revealing weapons. More of Reyes's armed guards.

Randy pulled Katherine behind a large cottonwood tree at the edge of the parking area. "Do you have your gun?"

She nodded. "In my ankle holster. You?"

"Yes." The gun Sheriff Walker had loaned him pressed against his back, providing little comfort against the number of weapons he'd seen displayed on the property so far. But he wouldn't voice those concerns to Katherine. No need to state the obvious.

There was a faint vibration sound, and Katherine pulled the prepaid cell phone out of her pocket. "Wanda got the warrant. They're headed this way. ETA forty-five minutes."

"Okay. Stay alert and meet me back here in thirty-five. If we don't find out anything by then, we'll lay low until our backup arrives."

She slipped out from behind the tree and headed toward the kitchen door.

"Lord, please, keep her safe," Randy whispered and took off toward the backyard at a casual pace.

There had to be at least fifty people buzzing around like worker bees. Some were decorating the tables in the large tent and arranging place settings. Others worked on attaching flowers to an arch that stood on a small platform at the end of an aisle, rows of chairs on each side. At the center of everything was an elderly woman dressed in a long purple dress, her white hair arranged elegantly on top of her head and her neck and fingers adorned with diamonds and pearls. The way she gave orders to those around her reminded Randy of his drill sergeants from boot camp, and he couldn't help but smile.

"What are you smiling at?" Uh-oh, she had spotted him hovering nearby.

"I'm sorry." He tilted his head in greeting. "I couldn't help but admire the way you take charge. Reminded me of someone from my past."

She leaned closer, her eyes narrowing. "Do I know you?"

"I don't believe I've had the pleasure. My name is Har—"

"No point telling me. I won't remember it more than a few minutes. Not because I'm senile, mind you." She waved her hand. "I'm just bad with names. What I really want to know is why are you in the backyard?"

"Oh." He cleared his throat. The best approach might be to stick as close to the truth as possible. "I'm looking for Victor."

"You must be one of the groomsmen. Why didn't you say so? My grandson is in the study with his father and brother. They aren't to be disturbed. No. Don't put that there. You'll block the view from the people sitting toward the back." She headed in the direction of a frazzled-looking man carrying a potted green shrub that had been cut into the shape of double hearts. Looking back over her shoulder at Randy, she pointed to the patio and the French doors that led into the house. "Get on upstairs and change into your tuxedo. The wedding starts in two hours. Pictures start in one."

She went back to giving orders to the workers. Randy scanned the area once more, noticing several photos of Victor and a dark-complected, dark-haired woman who must be the bride. Mandy had said every woman dreamed of her wedding day. Randy hated to be the reason for a bride's dream day to be shattered. Did the woman know about her fiancé's illegal business dealings? Whether she did or didn't, maybe she'd realize it was better to have a canceled wedding than to find herself married to someone who would be spending many years behind bars.

Randy headed toward the house, snagging one of the wedding programs off a table that also held a guest book. The guard barely glanced in Randy's direction as he walked past him. Apparently, if Victor's grandmother had given the order for him to enter the house, no one was going to question his right to be there.

Inside, another two dozen or so people bustled about, carrying a multitude of trays and things. The wedding party was upstairs. The groom and his father, and the unknown brother, were in the study. Randy headed down the hall. Footsteps approached from the opposite direction.

"Has anyone seen the groom? I can't believe he skipped out on his own bachelor party last night."

"Give him a break. His old man's in town. You know that always stresses him."

Randy ducked into a room under the stairs and found himself in a small lavatory. He locked the door and sank down onto the toilet.

The men in the hall walked past still discussing the control Xavier had over Victor. Randy examined the wedding program. Bride, Emilia Torres. Father of the bride, Antonio Torres. Best man, Arturo Reyes. Was that Victor's mysterious brother? Grandmother of the groom, Rosita Reyes. No wonder the property was so heavily guarded today. Xavier had a lot of enemies; he wouldn't want to risk the lives of his closest family members. Surprisingly, Trevor and Victor's mother wasn't listed on the program. Why wouldn't she be included in her son's wedding? Donna and Landon were also missing from the lineup. Wouldn't Victor want his sister-in-law and nephew in attendance for such a happy occasion?

Randy reached into the inside pocket of his blazer, withdrew the cell phone and powered it on. This constituted an emergency. Wanda needed to know what she and the other agents were driving toward. Maybe she could have someone at headquarters research the other families in the wedding party to determine if any of them were connected with the León Dormido Cartel or any other drug families.

Please, Lord, don't let the mole intercept this message. He typed a quick note, snapped a picture of the wedding program and sent it in a text message.

Opening the door, he poked his head out. All clear. He stepped into the hall and headed away from the main living area. If Randy had a study, he'd want it far away from the busy hub of the home. He imagined Victor would be the same.

He'd only taken a few steps when a guard headed toward him, his eyes fixed on Randy. He couldn't have identified him, but would most likely wonder why he was in this area. No sense taking chances.

"This isn't the way Abuela Rosita told me to go. I must have gotten turned around," he said loud enough for the guard to hear but soft enough to make it appear he was talking to himself.

He pivoted and came face-to-face with another guard blocking his path. This one was approximately six feet seven inches tall and had a muscular build. Randy glanced over his shoulder. The guard that stood behind him was twenty years older and a foot shorter than the one in front of him. The look on the older guard's face and his stance indicated he was the one in charge.

"Please come with us, Agent Ingalls," the older guard said, pulling back his jacket to reveal his weapon.

Randy's brain went into overdrive processing the situation. Could he go to battle against two guards and their weapons in a small hallway and win? Not likely. To fight now would simply waste his strength and tire him needlessly. Best to go along with the guards willingly and wait for an opportunity to escape to present itself. All he could do for now was pray Katherine was safe and hope Wanda would arrive soon with backup.

Katherine lunged forward to catch the radish that was rolling off the cutting board in an attempt to escape the knife in her hand.

"That's it!" The chef glared at her. "I don't know how you convinced Margaret that you were a sous-chef. You have done nothing but disrupt my kitchen. You're fired. Now, get out."

"Please, I really need this jo—"

"Mr. Reyes wants sandwiches and coffee brought to the study, immediately." A heavyset woman in a plain dark dress and black orthopedic shoes stood in the doorway, a glare on her face.

The chef huffed and threw a hand towel onto the counter. "I don't have time to make sandwiches. I barely have the staff needed to prepare the wedding dinner."

"You, standing there doing nothing." The woman pointed at Katherine. "Do you know how to make simple ham and cheese sandwiches?"

"Yes, ma'am."

"Fine. The bread is in the pantry. The other items you need are in the refrigerator. You have five minutes to brew a pot of coffee, make four sandwiches and load everything onto a tray." The woman glared at the chef. "I can't believe the mess you're making of my kitchen." She tsked and walked out of the room.

Katherine started the coffee and then rushed to gather the supplies for the sandwiches, ignoring the daggers the chef was throwing her way with his eyes.

Exactly five minutes later, one of the guards walked into the kitchen and nodded toward the tray. "Follow me."

All of the chattering in the room halted as she lifted the tray and trailed him out of the room. She puffed out her breath, slowly. To her knowledge, Xavier and Victor didn't know her. But if Torres was in the study, her cover would be blown. Where was Randy? The danger of separating on a mission was not having backup when needed.

The guard led her through the dining room, a large great room and down a long hallway. He stopped suddenly in front of a large double mahogany door, and she almost plowed into him. After glaring at her for the briefest second, he rapped his knuckles on the rich, dark wood. Someone inside the room gave the order to enter.

Praying no one would recognize her, Katherine cast her eyes downward as she entered the room.

"Place the items over there," the guard commanded, directing her to a sitting area tucked into a bay window.

She took her time unloading the contents of the tray onto the coffee table, all the while peering through her eyelashes at the four men in the study. Torres stood in the far corner, his back to the room as he surveyed the activity in the backyard. The dark-haired boss man from the cabin leaned against a bookcase, looking bored as he watched an older man and a younger man argue.

"I'm tired of this!" the older man who had to be Xavier exclaimed. "The whole point of bringing Arturo into the family business was to keep tabs on the feds. It's expensive to move the operation every time they get close."

"I know, Papa. I promise this will be the last move. Once we kill Ingalls and Lewis—"

"Once you kill them, you'll be on the FBI's most wanted list." The older man's face reddened; his fists clenched at his sides. "Do you really think they won't hunt you down after that?"

"The feds don't have anything to connect us to the crimes. We won't let them get close ever again." The younger man, obviously Victor, placed a hand on his father's arm only to have the older man shrug free. "Please, Papa. It's my wedding day."

"I don't care. I told you to postpone the wedding until after we fixed the mess your *brother* got us into."

"Wait a minute," the man from the cabin demanded and strode to the center of the room. "If anyone is responsible for this mess, it's Torres. Not me."

So, he was the brother. Uh-oh. At the mention of his name, Torres turned his attention back to the room. Time to go. Maybe she could hang around in the hall and eavesdrop since there hadn't been a guard stationed outside the door.

Katherine crossed the room, walking at a

steady pace so as to not draw unnecessary attention her way. *Schklikt.* The sound of a handgun being slid to load a cartridge into the chamber had the hairs on her neck standing at attention. The room got deathly quiet.

"Stop right there, Agent Lewis," Torres commanded.

She squared her shoulders, lifted her hands into the air and turned to face the handgun pointed at her head.

The guard frisked her, finding her cell phone and gun and tossing both to Victor. Katherine refused to flinch. Silently, she recited the memory verse Mom taught her when she was twelve and afraid of the dark, after sneaking and watching a horror movie. *What time I am afraid, I will trust in Thee. In God I will praise His word, in God I have put my trust; I will not fear what flesh can do unto me.*

"Coming here on my daughter's wedding day. I should kill you right now." Anger radiated off Torres as he attached a silencer to the barrel of his gun.

"Not in my study, Antonio. Too big of a mess to clean up." Victor put his hand on Torres's arm.

The phone on the desk rang, and Xavier answered it. He listened, then hung up and motioned for the boss man from the cabin to take hold of Katherine. "Arturo, take her to the old work shed behind the barn."

Xavier turned and smiled at her, not attempting to hide the gloating written all over his face. "So nice of you and Agent Ingalls to waltz in here and make capturing you so easy, Agent Lewis. You couldn't have given my son, or myself, a better present on his wedding day."

"The guards captured Randy?" Arturo asked, using her partner's first name as if they were the best of friends. She focused on the man holding on to her. His face had paled and sweat beaded his forehead. Randy had said he seemed familiar, but she didn't recognize him.

Xavier laughed. "Yes. And now, you get the honor of killing him. It's time you prove your loyalty to this family." The older man stretched to his full height, coming to stand in front of them and looking her captor in the eyes. "Otherwise, we'll have to dispose of you, too."

Katherine squirmed and tried to break free of Arturo's grasp.

"Fighting will only make it worse." To prove his point, Arturo tightened his grip, sending burning pain all the way down to her fingers.

Katherine stilled, and he loosened his grip just enough for the pain to lessen.

"Go with them, Victor. Make sure Arturo doesn't mess up this time." As head of the family, Xavier's command left no room for argument. "Make it fast. Oh, and don't get your suit dirty. Your wedding starts in less than two hours."

She was led out the French doors, into the backyard, and quickly ushered around the side of the house. Arturo flanked her on one side, while the guard who'd escorted her to the study flanked her on the other. Victor brought up the rear.

Lord, You are the beginning and the end, the Alpha and Omega. You know the outcome of the battle we are facing. I put all my trust in You.

A peace like none other she'd ever felt settled over Katherine. If they got out of this alive, she would have to thank Randy for helping her find her way back to the Lord. No, not if. When. Because she would fight with every ounce of her being to survive. Not only for Randy's life and hers, but for the lives of the people who were affected by the drugs the León Dormido Cartel filtered into the region every year. Failure was not an option.

The biggest guard held Randy, arms behind his back and kneeling on the hard cement floor. *Whack!* Randy's head snapped backward, the metallic taste of blood making him gag. The older guard had practiced his punching skills on Randy ever since he'd been brought into the vacant building behind the smaller of two barns on the property. His face ached, his right eye swollen nearly shut. If he could shake off the oversize giant who held him, Randy could take out the smaller man. He fought to wriggle free. The younger guard tightened his grip. Numbness started in Randy's hands and inched up his arms as the circulation was cut off.

The scraping sound of the metal garage door being slid open drew the guards' attention, offering a moment's respite. Randy rolled his head to the side for a better view. Four people stood in the opening, the sun behind them leaving their identities shrouded in shadows. They stepped into the windowless room, the old fluorescent fixtures casting a dim light over them. His heart skipped a beat. The boss man from the cabin and another guard held Katherine between them while Victor Reyes walked behind holding a gun on her. Randy sucked in a breath.

Katherine met his eyes, shock registering in hers. He tried to give her a look of reassurance but she didn't seem to be buying it. He didn't blame her. How reassuring could it be to see your partner a bloody, swollen mess?

The guard holding him pulled Randy to his feet, then released his hold and took a few steps back. They'd had their fun. The beating was over. It was time to silence Randy and Katherine forever. They would put a bullet between their eyes and dispose of their bodies.

SEVENTEEN

Randy fisted his hands. He itched to wipe the smug look off the face of the dark-haired man Torres had called boss at the cabin the other day. The man seemed so familiar. Why couldn't Randy remember his name?

Victor shoved Katherine into the room, pushing her into Randy. He stumbled but managed to stay upright, his arms wrapping around her protectively. "Are you okay?"

"Yes," she whispered with a slight nod.

"What a touching reunion." Victor laughed. "Seems you two have become very close. It's fitting you should die together."

"Let's just get this over with," the guard who had entered with Victor and the dark-haired man said. "Remember, your father warned you not to be late to your wedding."

Victor glared at the man. "I'll do as I please. This is my house. It is my day. And you will follow my orders." Turning to the other two guards, he added, "Now, all three of you, get back to the house. Arturo and I will handle this. It's the only way to guarantee it's done right."

The older guard who'd used Randy's face as a punching bag hesitated. "Mr. Reyes won't be—"

"You seem to forget who pays your salary. You answer to me, not my father. I said go. Now!" The guard gave a slight bow of his head and motioned for the other two to follow him out the door, closing it behind them.

This left Randy and Katherine alone with Victor and his brother. Xavier Reyes's other son.

"So, you're Victor's brother, Arturo Reyes." Randy studied the man who had remained silent since entering the building. The man was older than Victor, by ten to fifteen years at least. He would have been born long before Trevor's mom married Xavier. But Trevor never mentioned a stepbrother. Had Xavier kept this man a secret from Trevor's mom?

"Go ahead, Arturo. Introduce yourself." Victor smirked. "I think they deserve to know the man who's going to kill them."

"That isn't really necessary." Arturo pulled a gun out of his shoulder holster. "Let's just do this."

Randy inhaled sharply, his eyes narrowing.

Arturo sounded just like... No. It couldn't be. Randy's hearing must have been affected by all the hits he'd taken to the head a few moments ago.

The two brothers began a full-blown argument about who was in charge of the situation and how things would proceed. Although their guns were pointed in Randy and Katherine's general direction, Victor and Arturo faced each other in a typical sibling staring contest. The distraction was the perfect opening for Randy to take control.

He jerked his head in the men's direction. Katherine gave a slight nod. He mouthed, "You take Victor. On three. One. Two. Three."

He reached the end of his countdown, and Katherine lunged at Victor, tackling him in the side and sending him sprawling. Arturo focused his gaze toward Randy, lifting his gun to chest level. Before he could get a shot off, Randy did a roundhouse kick, sending the gun clattering across the floor. Arturo retaliated with a right hook, catching Randy in his already busted lip. Blood sprayed both their clothing.

Randy could hear Katherine and Victor fighting in the background. He desperately wanted to look to see if she was okay but knew he couldn't take his focus off his own fight. He had to subdue his opponent before he could help his partner. Executing a side kick, he caught Arturo in the ribs. He stumbled but didn't fall.

Angered, Arturo charged, punching Randy four times in the stomach, marching him backward with each hit. They reached the wall. Randy leaned backward, bracing his body against the solid surface, and kicked Arturo in the chest. Arturo flew ten feet or more through the air, landing on the hard concrete floor with a thud.

A black handle peeked out from behind a stack of crates in the corner beside an old workbench. The gun he'd kicked out of Arturo's hand. He took a step toward it, stopping midstride as the thunderous, deafening sound of a gunshot rang out. Whirling around, Randy's breath caught at the sight of Victor holding Katherine, his arm hooked around her neck and the barrel of his gun against her temple.

Clutching Victor's arm with both hands, Katherine wedged her fingers between her neck and the viselike grip that sought to cut off her oxygen. Randy met her gaze. There was no sign of panic in her eyes. *Good girl. Don't give up. We fight until the end.* As if she could read his thoughts, she blinked twice, rapidly, in agreement.

Victor kicked his brother's leg. "Get up off the floor. I would have thought you'd have enough training to be able to outmaneuver a federal agent. Pathetic."

"Don't blame me. It's your overeager guards' fault. Their beating only activated his adrenaline, giving him massive strength." Arturo stood and looked around. "Where's my gun?"

"You'll never find it in here. Too many boxes and things." Victor huffed. "I really need to clean out this old shed. Maybe tear it down. Or turn it into a workout space."

"Would you stop? This isn't the time to be making remodeling plans." Arturo extended his hand. "Now, give me your gun so we can end this once and for all."

A chill swept over Randy. He was transported back to the night of his accident, hidden behind a tree on a ledge on the side of the mountain as he listened to the conversation between Torres and a stranger on the road above.

"Looks like the world now has one less nosy cop," Torres laughed. *"One down, one to go."*

"You mean to tell me that not only did you lead him to me, but you haven't taken care of his partner yet?" a gravelly masculine voice demanded.

The voice was very distinct, with a strong Southern accent that seemed out of place.

Randy had the feeling he'd met the person speaking before, but he couldn't come up with the name that went with the voice.

"Boss, I promise, we have everything under control."

"No, you don't," the boss spat out, his disgust obvious. "That's why I'm here, to keep y'all from being arrested."

That voice. It sounded just like...

He turned his full attention to the so-called boss man who stood with Victor's gun pointed at Randy's chest. One brown eye and one blue studied him. Contact lenses. He clenched his teeth to keep from laughing at himself for not seeing through the disguise sooner. Remove the other colored lens, shave the beard and swap the hair from longish brown to a white-blond crew cut.

The reality of the situation hit him like a two-ton truck slamming into his chest at one hundred miles an hour. Xavier Reyes's mystery son, Arturo, was FBI Agent Trevor Douglas.

The man he'd loved like a brother had not only switched to the wrong side of the law but he also planned to kill Randy and Katherine.

"You can release Agent Lewis, Victor." Arturo laughed. "I can tell by the look on his face, Randy knows who I am now. He also knows he's out of time."

Victor released Katherine so suddenly she dropped to the floor with a thud. Pain shot up her leg, and she swallowed the yelp that begged to escape. She would not give the man the satisfaction of knowing he'd inflicted pain.

Randy was by her side in two strides. He grasped her upper arms and helped her stand. "Are you okay?"

"Yes." She glanced over her shoulder at the two brothers, Arturo looking strangely odd with one blue eye now. Turning back to Randy, she whispered, "What'd Arturo mean? Who is he?"

Deep, joyous laughter rang out, echoing in the building. "Go ahead, Randy. Tell your partner who I am."

She felt Randy stiffen as he pressed his lips tightly, his jaw set. The seconds ticked by. He took a deep breath and exhaled. "Arturo Reyes is an alias. The man pointing a gun at us is former FBI agent Trevor Douglas."

Katherine gasped. It couldn't be. Trevor? No wonder he'd seemed familiar to Randy. Her mind whirled.

"Your face is very expressive, Agent Lewis," Trevor drawled. "You're wondering how a law enforcement officer could turn his back on the law he'd sworn to uphold and turn to a life of crime."

"Yes, actually, I am." Keep him talking. Wanda was on her way with backup. The longer it took for him to get around to killing them, the better their chance of survival. "Please, explain it to me. Consider it as granting a condemned person's last wish. Since you're going to kill us, I'd really like to understand why."

"Do we really have time for this?" Victor asked impatiently.

Trevor shrugged. "I think it's important for Randy to understand it's his fault we've reached this point, not mine."

Anger bubbled inside Katherine. How dare Trevor try to make Randy feel guilty for his own actions. She opened her mouth to speak, but Randy squeezed her hand and gave a subtle shake of his head.

"I have no desire to hear you make excuses for your poor choices," Randy said casually.

Katherine would have believed his disinterest except for the slight twitch in his jaw. He was feigning indifference to encourage his former partner to talk longer.

"I didn't make a *poor choice*!" Trevor boomed. "I made the only choice. Victor and

Xavier were going after Landon. Grooming him to join the cartel."

"That's kind of what a drug cartel does," Katherine scoffed, unable to hold her tongue. "That's why it's our job to put the scumbags behind bars."

"That's it! I've had enough," Victor exploded. "Shoot them already. And let's get back to my wedding."

Trevor laughed. "Don't pay attention to Agent Lewis's insults. She's angry because her own brother was a drug addict who overdosed."

"How'd—" She swallowed the rest of her words as Randy's grip tightened. He was right. She shouldn't antagonize a man with a gun. *Focus, Katherine. You're trying to prolong the conversation, not speed up the shooting.*

"Oh, come now. Do you think I'd let my training go to waste?" Trevor sneered. "Of course I did a thorough background check on you. I needed to know who—besides my former partner—we were up against."

Randy shoved his hand through his hair, his first open sign of frustration.

"I don't understand. Instead of coming to me—so we could work together to put these monsters behind bars—you chose to join them, allowing them to continue to recruit other people's kids to push drugs. I would call that a poor choice on your part. How many families have had to suffer needlessly this past year after you sacrificed their children? All because you didn't trust me and the Bureau to keep Landon safe."

"That's right. I didn't trust you. Or the Bureau. Protecting Landon is my job." Trevor stepped closer, the barrel of the gun mere inches from Randy's chest. "And I'll never regret doing everything I can to keep him safe. Including shooting you."

Katherine wanted to knock the gun out of Trevor's hand, but one wrong move would get Randy killed. The last thing she wanted was to be responsible for the death of someone she loved.

"Chitchat time is over." Trevor stepped back and raised his weapon, pointing the barrel at Katherine's head. "What do you say, ladies first?"

Randy's chest tightened. No way was he going to sit back and watch Katherine be shot. "If you don't mind. I am curious about one more thing. Since we're going to die anyway, it can't hurt to tell us." He released Katherine's hand and turned. Trying to keep his movements relaxed and natural, he positioned his body so he stood halfway in front of her and fully faced Trevor. "It's about the mole working with you to help you stay a step ahead of the Bureau. Who is it? I can't figure out which one of our colleagues would betray us like that." Randy scoffed. "Other than you, that is."

Trevor's body shook as a deep, obviously joyous laughter overtook him. "I can't…" Ba-ha-ha-ha. "You seriously have no clue?" Ba-ha-ha.

Randy kept his face impassive and waited for his former partner to regain his composure.

"Oh, get a grip." Victor glared at Trevor, pulled his cell phone out of his pocket and punched in a number. "Come back to the shed," he barked and disconnected. Turning back to Trevor, he added, "If you don't kill them both this instant, my head of security will take care of it. And if he does, he'll kill you, too."

Trevor sobered, and straightened. "What's to stop me from killing you, little brother?"

Fear flashed in Victor's eyes for a brief second before he shuttered them. "If you kill me, you will be signing Landon's and Donna's death warrants. Xavier knows they're in Nebraska. You didn't really think we could hide them from him, did you?"

Randy could tell the instant Trevor realized he'd chosen the wrong side. Katherine placed a hand on Randy's back. She'd seen it, too. He could almost feel the hope radiating through her that Trevor wouldn't kill them and would instead take down Xavier and Victor. But Randy knew better. Trevor wasn't a person who freely admitted his mistakes. He would continue to be his brother's puppet.

"Stop making threats, Victor. I'm on your side. Remember?" Trevor smiled and his eyes glazed over, becoming icy in appearance. "I'll happily pull the trigger, but let me have a moment's joy of seeing the expression on my ex-partner's face when he discovers who the mole is."

"You have two minutes." Victor tapped his watch.

"I only need one." Trevor locked eyes with Randy. "You were the mole, feeding me the information of your whereabouts and helping us stay ahead of you."

Disbelief washed over him, and his eyes narrowed. "That's not possible."

"Isn't it?" Trevor pointed the gun at the watch on Randy's arm. "Why would I give you a valued family heirloom? Unless I needed you to have something you'd always wear."

The watch was a tracking device. Randy's wrist burned as if it had been branded. He yanked the offending device off his arm and slung it.

Trevor caught the watch with his free hand and examined the face. "It's not working. No wonder the signal has been spotty the past few days." Trevor looked back up. "Not the first time we've had issues with tracking, though, is it? You had to be all noble and give the watch to Landon. It took us a couple of months to figure out what had happened. We got signals from all up and down the Pacific Coast. At first, we thought you might have given up the chase and switched to a different case. Then the signal started coming from Omaha, and we figured out Landon had the watch.

"Victor reached out to Donna. You know, to check on her and Landon and to see how they were coping. He discovered they'd spent the summer traveling before settling into their new home close to her parents. Victor mentioned the watch and how he'd been upset I'd given the family heirloom to you, but then he'd realized how much you'd meant to me and that I must have really wanted you to have it to remember me by." He shook his head and laughed. "I knew she'd send it back to you. Of course, it took her a couple of months to do the right thing. Then it sat at the field office in Denver for another three months. By that time, y'all had already gotten jobs at Torres's ranch. Y'all were too close. There was no longer an option but to kill you. Only, Torres couldn't even get that right."

The metal garage door slid open, and the sound of sirens flooded the room, drawing Trevor's and Victor's attention. This was his chance. Randy dived for the gun he'd seen earlier, wrapped his hand around the handle and flipped to his back in a half sitting, half lying position.

Trevor smiled, lifted his gun and fired at Katherine. No! She fell backward against a stack of boxes, blood forming a red stain on the left side of her uniform. As if in slow motion, Trevor swung the gun in Randy's direction.

Switching his brain to autopilot, Randy aimed the weapon in his hand and pulled the trigger, hitting Trevor in the chest. Then he shifted his attention to the guard who'd entered a few seconds earlier.

"Freeze! Drop your weapon." FBI agents in bulletproof vests swarmed the building, taking Victor and his guard into custody before another shot could be fired.

Relief washed over him, and Randy scooted across the floor to Katherine. Yelling over his shoulder for someone to call an ambulance, he eased her head onto his lap. Her skin was pasty, and her breathing labored. Beads of sweat dotted her hairline. He felt for a pulse. "Hang in there. Help's on the way."

"You don't... I'm not dying," she said, her voice raspy. "He just nicked me." A smile lifted one corner of her mouth, drawing his own lips to hers as if by some magnetic force.

"Ahem." SAC Wanda Richardson looked down on the scene, an amused look on her face. Her eyes flicked to the wound on Katherine's side and she sobered. "Ambulance is en route. Ingalls, find me as soon as the EMTs take over here."

"But, I—" The do-not-argue-with-your-superior look on her face forced him to swallow the rest of his words. He nodded. "Yes, ma'am."

Less than five minutes later, two EMTs pushed their way through the throng of agents, making a beeline straight for Katherine.

"She was talking earlier, but she's been unconscious for the last several minutes. Her breathing is steady, and her heartbeat is strong."

"Thanks. We've got it from here." The female EMT jerked her head, indicating he needed to move.

Kissing Katherine's forehead, he whispered, "Please, Lord, let her be okay. I need her in my life." Then he relinquished his spot and reluctantly went to find Wanda.

She stood beside Trevor's lifeless body talking with a man wearing a windbreaker with the word *Coroner* emblazoned on it. Suddenly, Randy's feet felt like they were encased in cement. He couldn't take another step.

Wanda looked up, said something to the coroner and headed toward him. Putting a hand on Randy's shoulder, she guided him toward the exit. "Let's step outside."

At the door, he paused and looked back over his shoulder. The body of the man he had loved like a brother was being covered with a sheet. A year ago, Trevor had been given a hero's funeral. Randy had grieved his loss, feeling guilt over not being able to protect his partner from a cartel hit. But today, at this very moment, there was just anger.

Anger at Trevor for not trusting him and the Bureau to protect his family.

Anger at being forced to take the life of someone he had loved like a brother.

Anger that Trevor—a person who'd once been so honorable and caring—could change so drastically, in his own mind justifying turning from the light and joining the dark world of the cartel.

A feeling of dread descended upon Randy. How was he going to explain to Trevor's wife what had transpired here today?

EIGHTEEN

Katherine glanced at the clock hanging above the whiteboard that displayed pain-level emojis along with the names of her medical care team members and her medicine schedule for the umpteenth time. 9:37 a.m. Wanda would be here soon to pick her up.

Katherine was more than ready to go home. She had spent the past three days in the same hospital Randy had been in after his accident. At the thought of him, her chest tightened and tears stung the backs of her eyes. She hadn't seen him since the takedown, when Trevor had shot her. *Lord, I pray he's okay.* Of course, she knew he was okay physically. It was his emotional state that concerned her most. How was he holding up?

Picking up her cell phone that Wanda had dropped off yesterday with her clothes and shoes, she punched in Randy's number. Then, deleted it. She didn't even know if he'd gotten his phone replaced yet. If he had, wouldn't he have at least called to check on her?

Katherine sighed. Tossing back the cover, she swung her legs over the side of the bed and eased to a standing position. A sharp, burning sensation stabbed her left side. She gasped, holding her breath until the pain subsided.

Keeping her movements slow and steady, Katherine changed into a lightweight cotton turquoise floral-print dress. Then, she slid her feet into the open-back taupe sandals that sat on the floor, thankful Wanda had chosen loose-fitting clothing and easy-to-slip-on shoes.

The simple act of dressing was enough to make Katherine exhausted. Easing into the recliner positioned in front of the window, she watched as two robins flew past. The sun was shining and big, fluffy clouds floated in the sky, promising a beautiful spring day. A sudden feeling of homesickness washed over her. Maybe she should go visit Mom in Galveston, Texas. She'd have to take a medical leave until her doctor released her to return to work anyway. Might as well spend some of that time walking on the beach, her toes in the sand as she soaked up the sunshine and enjoyed the smell of salt water.

There was a knock at her door, and Sheriff

Walker poked his head into the room. "How's the patient feeling today?"

"Come on in, Sheriff." She smiled. "I'm surprised to see you here. I would have thought you'd be at your cabin or someplace relaxing to recover from your own gunshot wound."

"I figured you might like to swap *war stories*." He laughed as he entered the room, his arm in a sling. "But seriously, how are you?"

"Blessed to be alive. And thankful my injuries were minor."

"I don't know that I'd call being shot *minor*."

"Agreed. However, the doctor said the bullet more or less grazed my side. It cut a deep gash and brushed the outside of my rib cage, fracturing two of my ribs. If the bullet had hit just a couple of inches to the right, it would have been much worse." She shrugged. "I'll have a nasty scar once the stitches are removed, but with rest and time I'll make a complete recovery."

"Well, now, that is good news." He sat on the edge of the bed and faced her. "I had another reason for my visit today. I have a friend who's just been appointed to head up a new statewide drug task force. He's looking for a second-in-command. I thought of you. Would it be okay if I submitted your name for consideration?"

"I don't know what to say. I'm flattered, but—"

"Don't make a hasty decision," Sheriff Walker interrupted. "Take time to think about it. I saw you in action. You have a level head on your shoulders. I think you would be a good fit for the position."

Maybe he was right. The position would allow her to take a defensive role in eliminating illegal drugs versus the offensive role of an agent. Besides, hadn't she planned to ask for reassignment after they arrested Torres and the cartel?

"Have your friend contact me. I can at least listen to the job description and make an informed decision." She smiled. "But I'm headed out of town, so I won't be able to meet with him in person for the next couple of weeks."

"That's news to me. Wanda didn't say a word when I volunteered to pick you up."

Katherine startled at the sound of Randy's voice. He stood in the doorway, a shopping bag in one hand and a bouquet of pink roses and white daisies in the other.

"I just decided this morning." Did her voice sound as breathless to him as it did to her own ears? Her face warmed.

"Ahem. I'll take that as my cue to exit." Sheriff Walker headed to the door, stopping to shake Randy's hand. Then, glancing back at her, he added, "My friend will be in touch."

She nodded, never taking her eyes off Randy. The smile on his face couldn't erase the dark circles or the look of exhaustion in his eyes.

"How are—" they said in unison.

Randy came closer. "I'm fine. You look surprisingly rested."

"Well, you know. Pain meds tend to help with sleep." Katherine tilted her head. "The flowers are beautiful."

"Oh, yeah. These are for you." He handed them to her.

She inhaled their sweet scent and smiled, eyeing the bag in his hand that bore the name of a chain department store. "Let me guess. Those are replacement clothes for the ones you took from the orderly's locker."

"I thought about sending him money, but decided buying the items myself would save him from having to go shopping." He shrugged. "I'll drop them off at the nurses' station when you're discharged."

His thoughtfulness didn't surprise her. She imagined he'd been doing a lot of thoughtful things the past few days. Trying to right wrongs. Silence descended on the room.

Randy remained standing as if he were

afraid of getting near her. She waited, not wanting to rush him. Whatever had taken him so long to come visit needed to be shared in his own time, not hers. Just seeing him, knowing he was safe, filled her heart with joy. Katherine wanted to relish this moment, especially if, as she feared, he was there to tell her they could only be friends and nothing more.

Randy pulled to a stop in front of Katherine's condo in Denver. The ride had been completed in relative silence. Katherine had fallen asleep twenty minutes into the drive, which had been fine with him. He had needed the extra time to get his thoughts together. The sight of her in the hospital room had been almost more than he could bear. The urge to sweep her up into a protective hug had been so strong, only Sheriff Walker's presence had prevented him from embarrassing himself. A hospital didn't offer the privacy needed for the talk he had planned.

Putting the vehicle into Park, he turned off the engine and glanced toward Katherine. She was still sleeping. Her head was leaned against the seat, and her brown, wavy hair fell like a drape across her face. Instinctively, he reached out and tucked the hair behind her ear.

She startled, saw him and smiled. "Hi."

"Hi, yourself." He leaned closer and kissed her forehead. "You're home. Let's get you inside."

Not waiting for a reply, he exited the vehicle and hurried to open her door, offering his arm for her to lean on. A smile lifted the corners of his mouth. If she would allow him to do so, he would happily spend the rest of his life being her support.

Soon, Katherine was settled on the couch, and Randy went to the kitchen to see what he could find to prepare for lunch. The fridge was empty, except for a jar of pickles, some condiments and a few cans of cola. Should he place a grocery delivery order? She'd told the sheriff she was headed out of town for a few weeks.

"What do you like on your pizza?" Katherine yelled from the living room.

He crossed to the doorway. "As long as it doesn't have anchovies or pineapples, I'm good with anything."

She smiled and gave her order to the person on the other end of the phone, then disconnected. "They said it'd be here in twenty minutes."

"Do you want me to run to the grocery store and pick up a few things?"

"No need. I'm going to my mom's." She motioned for him to sit beside her. "Tell me what you've been doing the last few days."

"I'm sorry I didn't make it to the hospital sooner." Settling on the couch beside her, he took a deep breath and puffed it out. How could he explain that his absence hadn't meant she wasn't a priority in his life? He'd had an obligation to see the case to the end.

Katherine reached over and took his hand in hers. "It couldn't have been easy to tell Trevor's wife what happened."

"How did you know that's where I was?"

She smiled. "Because I know you. You're an honorable man. I'm sure you felt it was your responsibility to go see her in person."

His throat tightened at the memory of his meeting with Donna the day before. Not wanting to keep something so personal from Katherine, he related as much of the encounter as he could stand to relive. "She doesn't want Landon to know the truth."

"Do you think that's wise?"

"It's not up to me. She said she buried her husband a year ago, and she wasn't going to bury him again. I can't say I blame her." He shrugged. "Wanda had someone remove the tracking device from the watch. I had it repaired and gave it to Donna for Landon."

"That's nice. It's important to have good

memories of the past." She bit her lip. "I'm sorry for being a standoffish partner before your accident. I used to think you liked giving orders, not discussing things with me or letting me have a say in how things were handled. Now, I realize the reason I wasn't treated like a partner was because I wasn't acting like one."

He laced his fingers with hers and waited for her to continue.

"When I went to the academy, I dated another trainee. By the time the twenty weeks were up, we had mapped out our entire future together. He proposed, and we planned a big wedding in my hometown. Almost everyone in town showed up. Everyone except…the groom. He left me a note telling me he had decided it would be too hard to be married to another agent. We would be working different assignments and having a quality family life would be almost impossible."

Randy wanted to say something to comfort her, but the words stuck in his throat. He couldn't understand anyone not doing everything they could to have a life with the person they loved.

"Being left at the altar was painful. And then having to face everyone at work, knowing they felt sorry for me, and being the topic of gossip at the coffee machine, it was too much. After that, I made a vow to keep my personal life and work life separate. I would do my job, without forming close friendships. And I'd never date a coworker again."

Her words hit him like a sucker punch to the gut. He couldn't let her just walk out of his life. "But, that—"

"Then you came along. Or should I say Mac did." She smiled, placing her free hand against his cheek. "I put my guard down, and you crept into my heart. Now, I can't imagine my life without you in it."

"Good. Because I don't plan on going anywhere." He grasped the hand that rested against his face and kissed her palm. "I love you, and I want to date you. And when the time's right, plan a future with you."

"I love you, too." Tears of joy glistened in her eyes, and she laughed. "And if I take the job with the new drug task force, we won't be coworkers anymore."

"Coworkers. Conflicting work schedules. Or anything else. Nothing will cause me to give up on us." He leaned close, his eyes never leaving hers.

There was a knock at the door. "Pizza delivery."

He smiled. The pizza guy would just have

to wait. Randy lowered his head and savored the sweet taste of her lips. *Thank You, Lord, for helping me find home.*

EPILOGUE

Katherine lifted the bouquet of pink roses and white daisies, inhaling their sweet scent as her mind drifted back to that day in the hospital eighteen months ago when Randy had brought her an almost identical bouquet.

"You know, you don't have to bring me flowers every time you return home from an assignment. Simply seeing you walk through that door, safe and sound, is the only gift I need for the rest of my life."

"I like getting you flowers. I know how much you enjoy them." He shrugged. "Besides, I didn't get you any for our anniversary last month."

"No, but you took me to Hawaii for our belated honeymoon." Katherine had felt horrible when she couldn't take time off from her new job with the drug task force for a honeymoon, but Randy had been so understanding and promised to take her on a nice trip for their first anniversary.

The timing of their recent vacation couldn't have been better as their lives were about to change in a marvelous way. Katherine was bursting to tell her husband, but she'd planned a special dinner to share the joyous news so she'd have to wait a few more hours. She lifted her face for a kiss.

His lips touched hers, and she melted into his arms. Cellophane wrapping crinkled as the flowers were crushed between them. She jumped back and smiled. "I better get these into some water."

Randy put a hand on her arm, stopping her. "Not until you tell me how the appointment went with your doctor. Did she have any idea what's causing your migraines? What's the treatment plan?"

The concern in his eyes made her heart swell. If someone would have told her that she could ever love this man more than she had the day they'd said "I do," she never would have believed them. How would her heart be able to handle all the love that would grow inside it over the next months, years, decades? *Thank You, Lord, for blessing me more than I deserve.*

Katherine placed the flowers on the entryway table and led her husband to his oversize recliner. He needed to be seated before she could share what the doctor had discovered.

"Okay, you're starting to scare me. How seriously ill are you? I don't want you to worry about a thing." He sat down, pulling her onto his lap in a tight hug. "I'll find you the best doctors. Even if it means—"

She placed a finger on his lips, silencing him. "Would you give me a chance to tell you what the doctor said? I don't know why you have to jump to worst-case scenario right off the bat. Even when we were on the run from the cartel and your memory hadn't returned, you thought we were spies or something equally as bad."

"You're right. I'm sorry. I love you so much, and I want you to be okay." He took a deep breath and released it slowly. "So, what's causing the headaches and how do we make them stop?"

"Dr. Elmore said the migraines aren't anything to worry about. She told me to take acetaminophen and make sure I'm drinking lots of water to stay well hydrated."

"That's it? Over-the-counter pain meds and water will cure the horrific headaches you've suffered the past couple of weeks?"

She smiled. "Well, that and time. Dr. Elmore

said the headaches should lessen and hopefully stop completely in a few months." Katherine searched his face, not wanting to miss the moment her words sank in. "It's common for women to experience headaches and migraines in the first trimester while their body is experiencing an influx of hormones."

"Trimester?" He jumped up, lifting her with him, and swung her around in an excited hug. "You're having a baby!"

"Correction." She pulled back and smiled. "*We're* having a baby."

A smile lit his face. "Thank You, Lord, for blessing us with this amazing gift," he said aloud before lowering his head and claiming her lips in a sweet, tender kiss.

Katherine's life may not have followed the path she had planned, but she knew she was right where she belonged.

* * * * *

If you liked this story from Rhonda Starnes, check out her previous Love Inspired Suspense book:

Rocky Mountain Revenge

Find more great reads at www.LoveInspired.com.

Dear Reader,

I hope you enjoyed reading Randy and Katherine's story as much as I enjoyed writing it. I must confess, life threw a couple of curveballs my way while writing this story. Like Randy did in the story when he didn't let his lost memories keep him from doing his job, I had to learn to let go of things I couldn't control.

Some days writing was hard, but each day I was reminded, no matter what's going on in life, we are never alone. God is there to carry us through the difficult times. We simply have to follow His will and lean on Him for support, the way Katherine learned to do.

Thank you for being part of my writing journey. I would love to hear from you. Please, connect with me at www.rhondastarnes.com or find me on Facebook @AuthorRhondaStarnes.

All my best,
Rhonda Starnes

Get 4 FREE REWARDS!

We'll send you 2 FREE Books plus 2 FREE Mystery Gifts.

FREE Value Over **$20**

Both the **Harlequin® Special Edition** and **Harlequin® Heartwarming™** series feature compelling novels filled with stories of love and strength where the bonds of friendship, family and community unite.

YES! Please send me 2 FREE novels from the Harlequin Special Edition or Harlequin Heartwarming series and my 2 FREE gifts (gifts are worth about $10 retail). After receiving them, if I don't wish to receive any more books, I can return the shipping statement marked "cancel." If I don't cancel, I will receive 6 brand-new Harlequin Special Edition books every month and be billed just $4.99 each in the U.S or $5.74 each in Canada, a savings of at least 17% off the cover price or 4 brand-new Harlequin Heartwarming Larger-Print books every month and be billed just $5.74 each in the U.S. or $6.24 each in Canada, a savings of at least 21% off the cover price. It's quite a bargain! Shipping and handling is just 50¢ per book in the U.S. and $1.25 per book in Canada.* I understand that accepting the 2 free books and gifts places me under no obligation to buy anything. I can always return a shipment and cancel at any time. The free books and gifts are mine to keep no matter what I decide.

Choose one: ☐ **Harlequin Special Edition**   ☐ **Harlequin Heartwarming**
  (235/335 HDN GNMP)   **Larger-Print**
                 (161/361 HDN GNPZ)

Name (please print)

Address   Apt. #

City   State/Province   Zip/Postal Code

Email: Please check this box ☐ if you would like to receive newsletters and promotional emails from Harlequin Enterprises ULC and its affiliates. You can unsubscribe anytime.

Mail to the **Harlequin Reader Service:**
IN U.S.A.: P.O. Box 1341, Buffalo, NY 14240-8531
IN CANADA: P.O. Box 603, Fort Erie, Ontario L2A 5X3

Want to try 2 free books from another series! Call 1-800-873-8635 or visit www.ReaderService.com.

---

*Terms and prices subject to change without notice. Prices do not include sales taxes, which will be charged (if applicable) based on your state or country of residence. Canadian residents will be charged applicable taxes. Offer not valid in Quebec. This offer is limited to one order per household. Books received may not be as shown. Not valid for current subscribers to the Harlequin Special Edition or Harlequin Heartwarming series. All orders subject to approval. Credit or debit balances in a customer's account(s) may be offset by any other outstanding balance owed by or to the customer. Please allow 4 to 6 weeks for delivery. Offer available while quantities last.

Your Privacy—Your information is being collected by Harlequin Enterprises ULC, operating as Harlequin Reader Service. For a complete summary of the information we collect, how we use this information and to whom it is disclosed, please visit our privacy notice located at corporate.harlequin.com/privacy-notice. From time to time we may also exchange your personal information with reputable third parties. If you wish to opt out of this sharing of your personal information, please visit readerservice.com/consumerschoice or call 1-800-873-8635. **Notice to California Residents**—Under California law, you have specific rights to control and access your data. For more information on these rights and how to exercise them, visit corporate.harlequin.com/california-privacy.

HSEHW22

COUNTRY LEGACY COLLECTION